D1320037

To My Pal, Muriel
From Betty

1941

Alice took her first picture.

MARY JANE IN SWITZERLAND

BY
CLARA INGRAM JUDSON

GROSSET & DUNLAP
PUBLISHERS   NEW YORK

Printed in the United States of America

CONTENTS

ILLUSTRATIONS

MARY JANE IN SWITZERLAND

GOOD-BY TO PARIS

MARY JANE sat at the window of her room in the hotel in Paris and carefully counted her postal cards. There were twenty-two—all of streets or buildings she had seen during these days of sight-seeing. And at one side of the pile were three packs of folding pictures showing the whole city and more of the buildings and boulevards.

"There now," Mary Jane said with a satisfied sigh, "I guess I really have enough. Now I'll have to see about my souvenirs." She proceeded to count off the various things she had purchased and to fold them back in their tissue paper wrappings after she had made sure they were as she remembered them. Then she counted gifts she had bought and was just wrapping them up when her mother stepped to the door of her room.

"My dear!' Up so early?" she exclaimed. "I was just going to call you."

"I waked up, mother, because I wanted to see if I had to buy any more cards. I guess that waked me. Or else it was the taxis. Anyway, I've enough cards so you can pack them now."

"That's fine," said her mother appreciatively, "for with all the packing we didn't finish last night and dressing and breakfast, two hours won't be a minute too much for us, I know.

"Now if you'll call Alice and then take your tub, dear," she continued, "I'll ring for our breakfast and we'll be ready for it when it arrives."

Mary Jane tossed a pillow over to her sleeping sister and followed it up with such a vigorous shake that Alice simply couldn't help waking up. Then she ran to the bath room where sounds of splashing and soaping soon told that she would be clean for the start of her long journey.

It was a good thing that she waked up early, for then she had time to linger over the rolls and jam and chocolate which were waiting on the table when she was dressed. The Merrills had decided to leave their trunks in Paris and take only hand luggage on their journey to Switzerland and Italy so all their heavy clothing and souvenirs had to be packed while summer frocks and shoes went in the grips. But with everyone helping, they had everything done and were gathering up hats, camera, and bags when the boy came to tell them that their taxi was waiting. And it was even then only seven-thirty, so you see they really were very speedy.

While they drive through the freshly scrubbed street of Paris this fine morning in late July perhaps we had better stop and tell some of our readers who these girls are. Those of you who have read the Mary Jane books thus far are old friends, but the rest of you will want to know something about the travelers.

Alice and Mary Jane Merrill, with their mother and father, left their home in Chicago as soon as school closed in June. Since then they have had a beautiful time traveling. They crossed the ocean on a big liner, arriving in Plymouth, and from there they toured England and Scotland where they saw many beautiful sights and had many interesting adventures. Then they went to France and in a few busy days saw much of Paris, the battlefields of the World War, and some of the many fine castles near Paris. Of course they cannot stop as long at any one place as they would enjoy doing, for they must be back for school in the fall and they want to get a glimpse of several countries while they are across. Perhaps some

other time they can come again and live a
whole summer in each country and see all
the interesting sights and customs.   But
now they are having great fun dashing
about and they are so used to strange foods,
hasty packing, catching trains and such that
Mary Jane begins to feel like a very experienced traveler.

"How long will we be on the train?"
asked Alice as their driver pulled up with a
jerk at the great station and Mr. Merrill
motioned to a porter to take their bags.

"All day long," replied Mrs. Merrill,
"and something tells me that it's going to
be a hot day, too.   I looked at the time-table
yesterday and found that we arrive in Montreux at seven thirty-five—nineteen thirty-
five they call it—almost a twelve-hour trip."

"Don't you wish we could have a compartment all to ourselves and have a lunch
like one we would pack at home?" asked
Mary Jane.   "We could pretend to keep
house and eat when we pleased.   Remember

how tippy that restaurant car was when we rode from Calais to Paris? I never knew where my mouth was going to be by the time I got the food up to it—no, really, Alice," she added as she saw she was being laughed at, "I never did!"

"I didn't either, Pussy," agreed Alice, "but you say it so comically that I had to laugh. Maybe we could have brought some lunches from that nice place near the hotel."

"Too late to think of that now," Mr. Merrill reminded them as they followed their porters through the station. "Let's get aboard quickly and get settled before the last minute crowd arrives."

They found their reserved places quickly enough and Mary Jane was soon settled by the window. Between looking at the pictures on the wall in the compartment and watching the people coming and going outside, she was much entertained. The pictures with their curious looking French inscriptions showed very pretty scenes in

France and Switzerland. Mary Jane resolved that before she came to Europe next time she would learn French so she could read such things. There were some directions to travelers which appeared in French, English and German, and she read those and tried to find the words in French to correspond with the English ones she knew.

"Look, Alice," she said, pulling at Alice's arm to attract her attention, "they say not to throw anything out of the window or we'll be arrested. Isn't that a funny notice? What would we throw and where?"

"Oh, papers, maybe, or anything," replied Alice, not really thinking. "Look, Mary Jane! There's an old woman selling boxes of something. She's coming by here! Dadah! I believe she's selling box lunches!"

"Oh, could we buy some?" cried Mary Jane, gleefully. "That's just what we were wanting to have! Isn't it lucky she came our way?"

Mr. Merrill was uncertain whether box lunches would be good and reminded the girls that a restaurant car was on the train. But while they were talking the old woman noticed their interest and came to the window to urge them to buy.

"Luncheon basket?" she asked, "luncheon basket for the journey?"

"Good lunch," she assured them in easily understood English. "Bread, meat, fruit. Best luncheon basket. Five francs. Good lunch for the little ladies."

"Do get some, Dadah," said Mary Jane, "it'll be lots more fun than eating in the big diner."

"That's the first time I ever heard you try to avoid a diner, Mary Jane," laughed her father. "If you're willing to try a box lunch, 'luncheon basket,' she calls it, I guess the rest of us can too. Here, we'll take four!" Grinning broadly the old woman sold the lunches through the open window and the girls climbed up and put the boxes in the rack overhead just as the train started to move.

The first hour out of Paris was lots of fun. The girls could get glimpses of spotlessly clean streets, stone and plaster houses, and here and there a park or ground of an estate. By the end of the hour, Paris and everything near it was well behind them and they were riding through open country—very much the same sort of country as in New York state, the girls thought. There were some particular differences, to be sure—roads lined with double rows of trees, many tiny canals also with trees on each side their slowly flowing water, bicycles instead of cars on many roads, many pretty little villages and scores of beautiful chapels and churches.

At first Mary Jane tried to count them all but that kept her so busy running between the corridor window on one side and the window by her own seat that at last she gave it up.

"Suppose instead of running around the train, you sit here and see where we are going," suggested Mr. Merrill. He pulled down a suit-case and set it up across Alice's and Mary Jane's knees like a table and on it he spread a map of Switzerland.

"Now then," said he, pointing with his pencil, "here is about where we are now. And way down here, at Montreux, is where we shall eat dinner this evening."

"Goodness!" cried Alice, "no wonder it's a long ride." And no wonder indeed, as you can see if you will get a map yourself and see where the girls were to go.

"Then from Montreux," he continued, tracing with his pencil, "we shall go to Interlaken."

"But there are pretty high mountains in between," said Mary Jane, doubtfully. "They show very black on the map. What shall we do about those?"

"We'll go around some and up and down

some," promised her father. "You just wait and see."

"*Up* a mountain?" asked Mary Jane, wonderingly.

"Right up the side of the mountain," repeated her father.

"Will there be tunnels?" inquired Alice.

"Lots of them, and black as midnight. Oh, you'll have traveling that's fun in Switzerland, I promise you that.

"Then," he continued, "from Interlaken we'll go way over here to Lucerne and then down south to Lugano. So, though you'll see only a little of all the sights of Switzerland, you'll still have variety enough to know something about this wonderful country."

Mary Jane and Alice studied that map for an hour, marking with crosses the places they were to stop and finding pictures in the compartment and in guide books of places they were to see. Then they put the map away for safe keeping and looked out of the windows again.

By eleven o'clock they were hot, hungry, and thirsty, and as there was no water in the train for thirsty travelers, Mary Jane suddenly remembered the luncheon baskets and that they had been said to contain water.

"Let's have our luncheon now," she suggested eagerly, as she smacked her dry lips and anticipated a delicious feast in those covered boxes. "There's water—and wine, mother—and you know you said we might taste some of that sometime. And I didn't eat nearly enough for breakfast, I was in such a hurry!"

"That was your mistake, Pussy," laughed her father. "How about those rolls? Did you eat two or three? I seem to forget."

"And I do, too," laughed Mary Jane, "but really, Dadah, that was a long time ago—seven o'clock it was."

"So is dinner time a long time away," said Mr. Merrill, darkly. "Such a long time that I hate to think of what may happen to a little girl who will eat her luncheon so early. But I see they are beginning to call the first sitting for luncheon on the train, so perhaps we can manage. Anyway, you got the luncheon baskets for an experiment. Let's open them and see what we find."

Gleefully Mary Jane climbed up on the seat so she could reach the luggage rack overhead and then handed down to Alice the four little luncheon baskets. They really were not baskets at all, but boxes of thinnest pasteboard tied with string.

As she handled them so carefully, she thought delightedly of all the nice lunches she had ever seen—and there were a good many. She half way expected to discover that some good fairy had put *all* those good lunches inside the four boxes—which, of course, no fairy had. When she opened it, Mary Jane found in her box a small paper napkin, two small bottles, one filled with water and one with red wine, two very thick sandwiches, and a very ripe banana. A bottle opener and a tiny tin knife, fork, and spoon were the things that had made the interesting rattle when the box was moved.

Mary Jane looked carefully at her basket, peeped to see that the other three had the same uninteresting looking contents, and then remarked bravely, "Maybe it tastes better than it looks."

"Maybe it does," agreed Alice, "and here goes." Whereupon she took a bite of the biggest sandwich—a cheese one.

The thick, firm bread was not attractive looking, the cheese was cut in thick slabs, and there was no butter; but just the same, Mary Jane was really hungry and the food was clean and wholesome. So she took a sampling bite and then ate right straight through that whole big sandwich, crust and all.

"Now, if only the water is good," she said, as she got out her own little drinking cup, took the cap off the bottle, and poured a cupful. But alas, she had forgotten that it was a hot summer day for the water as well as for little girls! The water was warm, almost warm enough to make into tea, it seemed. Alice tried the wine, but of course it was just as warm, sour as well, and not one bit to her taste.

"Whatever shall we do with the bottles?" asked Alice, looking in distress at the two which were now open and almost full.

"I'm going to drink all my water," decided Mary Jane, "and then I'll hold the wine bottle between my feet while I eat my other sandwich and banana."

But holding an opened bottle of red wine between your feet while a train dashes across the country is not as easy as it may sound, Mary Jane discovered. By the time she had finished her luncheon she was tired of the job.

"It splashes and spills no matter how I hold it," she complained, "and I'm going to do *something!* Let's get them all in a row,

Alice—empty water ones and the wine ones. Then we'll throw them out the window."

The English ladies had long since gone to the restaurant car for their luncheon and Mr. and Mrs. Merrill had left the girls alone while they went to explore the possibilities of getting a cool drink without a big hot dinner. The girls decided to get rid of the troublesome bottles and tidy the compartment while they were freer to move about than they were when it was filled with six people.

Alice raised one window enough to allow a bottle to be tossed out; then, steadying them carefully all the while, they put the bottles in a row just below the sill.

"There now," she said, much pleased with her work, "I'll look out ahead and be sure it's all right to throw and you toss four of them out. Then we'll change places and you watch."

That seemed good sport and Mary Jane

quite forgot about being thirsty or tired.
When Alice said "Now!" she tossed out the
first bottle as quickly as she could; then the
second; then the third and fourth. She just
reached for the fifth when the sudden
grinding of brakes threw her off her seat
into Alice's lap—fortunately with an empty
water bottle, the partly filled wine bottles
having been the first to go.

"What's happened?" she cried, rubbing
her elbows. "There isn't any city. There
isn't even a village. We're stopping right
in the middle of a field! Do you suppose
it's a wreck, Alice?"

Alice steadied her sister tenderly and
made sure that her arm was not really in-
jured, then as she turned to sit down again
she happened to glance above Mary Jane's
head to the signs they had been idly reading before lunch.

"Mary Jane," she whispered in awe-
struck tones, "that sign says 'Do not throw
anything from the train.' We forgot. Do

you suppose that's why the train has stopped? It must be! Do you suppose they are coming to arrest us *now?*"

With startled, white faces the girls looked at the door of the compartment, expecting they knew not what to happen.

SEEING MONTREUX

TRAIN men hurrying through the car and talking together in excited French certainly did not reassure the two frightened girls. Indeed, their faces were so white and strained that if the men had not been in haste and more than usually busy with their own affairs they might have noticed that something was wrong and stopped to inquire what the trouble was. But fortunately they didn't. No one else went by.

For a few minutes—really a very few minutes, although it seemed a long, long time to Mary Jane—the train stood still. The girls felt so guilty that they hardly dared breathe. Then, slowly at first, the train began to move. Mary Jane pressed her face against the windowpane and saw gangs of workmen repairing the track on ahead. As the train approached, the workmen stepped back and very slowly the train crawled by.

"I think we stopped on account of the workmen, not on account of our throwing out the bottles," whispered Alice, when the train began to gather speed as the working crew was passed.

"Do you *really*, Alice?" exclaimed Mary Jane, in such relief that rosy color came back into her face. "But it does say 'Do not throw anything from the window.' It says so in big letters."

"Yes, it does," agreed Alice, "and we ought to have remembered because we read it plainly enough. I suppose that sign is put there on account of the men working on the road. Just suppose we had waited half a minute to throw out our bottles and they had hit someone. I guess the train wouldn't have started till they found who did *that!*"

"But we looked before I threw them," Mary Jane reminded her.

"And a good thing we did, too," agreed Alice. "But it was a narrow escape all the same and I say we let the rest of the bottles stay on the floor. They can clatter if they like but we'll not throw them out—not we!"

Mary Jane agreed hastily, and the girls arranged the bottles out of sight under the seat and in great relief settled themselves to looking at pictures and maps.

When Mr. and Mrs. Merrill returned to the compartment a few minutes later, they were much interested in hearing about the bad scare the girls had had. They agreed that rules had better be obeyed exactly, not only because there was probably a good reason for the rule but because it would save worry to visitors who did not know the language and who might have many difficulties in case a misunderstanding came up.

"But did you find anything for us to

drink?" asked Mary Jane. Visions of a tall cold glass of iced lemonade she had once enjoyed on a train came to her mind.

"No," replied her father, "but I found we could have tea at three o'clock and as all the sittings for luncheon are sold now, that's the best we can do. It won't be long now till three, so let's sit very comfortably and watch the roads and villages."

The English ladies came back just then and very plainly made ready to take a nap and so Mary Jane resolved to be very, very quiet. If she slept a little, too—well, probably it was just as well, for it *was* a hot day, you know.

"First sitting for tea!" called a pleasant voice. Of course the words were said in French but Mary Jane had long ere this learned to recognize "tea" and "first" and a few other often used words so she had no difficulty in knowing what was said.

"Let's go right away!" she exclaimed, so she and Alice made themselves as tidy as possible and then all four went into the restaurant car. There they had a very good and generous tea, with English tea cake, toasted muffins, delicious French pastries and a most interested and obliging waiter to see that they had everything they wanted. The car was nearly empty so they did not have to hurry. Somehow cakes and fruit and tea things seemed much easier to eat on the fast moving train than soup that one must "spoon" up and meat that had to be cut. So the tea party was quite a success. Mary Jane ended up by being very glad they had tried the luncheon baskets because they had had the fun of seeing what they contained, the excitement of disposing of the troublesome bottles and then, best of all, the good tea.

The rest of the afternoon seemed to pass more quickly. There were many villages and some small cities; the border of Switzerland was passed with little formality with the customs and soon the party reached Lausanne which was fun to see because it was right on lovely Lake Geneva, and because there were so many young people at the station. The English ladies told Mary Jane that Lausanne had many fine schools and that that was the reason why so many children and young people were about. But even though it was more interesting to ride along the lake past many a town and through many a tunnel, none the less Mary Jane and Alice were very glad when they reached Montreux and it was time to get off.

The train left them on a broad platform level with the roof of a great hotel. Behind was a mountain that went up to the clouds. In front, over the top of the hotel, were more clouds with a glimpse between buildings of a lake very near by. Off to the west was another hotel, not nearly so big but on the same level as the station. Mary Jane was just spelling out the sign when a great tall man stepped up to them and said in very nice English, "Mr. Merrill?"

Mr. Merrill replied quickly and Mary Jane beamed with delight. It *was* nice when arriving tired and hot in a strange country to find that someone expected you. The man picked up the Merrill's bags and tucked them under his arms as though they were mere trifles (which they certainly were *not*—they were heavy!) and started off toward the hotel. As it was only a few hundred feet away, it was easier to walk than to get in and out of a cab so the four Merrils followed briskly along, glad of a chance to stretch cramped muscles.

The hotel was small and had a tiny little parlor and a winding stair going up from the entry. The Merrills went up two flights and then turned down a hall and into a suite that was anything but small. Two lovely adjoining rooms and each opening out on a big porch seemed more like an apartment than hotel rooms. The girls ran around exploring in high glee. From the porch they could look right over the roofs of buildings to the lake, but there wasn't a mountain to be seen anywhere. This seemed funny as they had expected to see some high ones. A knock at the door interrupted investigations and a neat little maid brought in two great pitchers of steaming hot water.

That led to scrubbing and reminded the girls that dinner could be enjoyed whenever they were ready for it. That was even more interesting than a hunt for missing mountains.

It was exactly eight when they were ready but that didn't seem surprising to anyone and the dining room was still comfortably filled with guests. On the way down stairs to the dining room on the second floor, Mary Jane sniffed some delicious odors and as they turned at the second floor she saw where they came from. One of the two doors at the landing was wide open, showing a tiny little kitchen—more like the kitchen on a Pullman diner than anything else she had ever seen. A wide bar was let down instead of the door and behind this bar the man who had carried their bags, transformed by a spotless apron and great white cap, stood cooking their dinner.

He grinned at them gaily and with an experienced hand flipped some potatoes from griddle to dish as he said, "Ready for your dinner? You must have what you like!"

And they certainly did, from fruits to begin with to cheeses at the end. By that time dark had come and the maid brought funny little candles in carved wooden holders to light their way through the dessert course. By that time the dining room was empty and the cook came in to make sure they were getting all they wished. They learned from his talk that the hotel was so small that it was run entirely by this man, his wife, and their two children. The man was cook and porter by turns and the mother was maid and waitress. The children, a boy and a girl just between the ages of Alice and Mary Jane, scurried around removing dishes, lighting candles, and making themselves useful. The next morning the girls saw them polishing silver and rubbing the windows of the dining room till they sparkled, but the boy and girl were so very shy that not a word was heard from them all the time the Merrills were in Montreux.

After dinner Mr. Merrill suggested a walk, and so all climbed down the hillside road to the lake level where they saw the front of the great hotel whose roof they had already seen. Its porches and walks and gardens were lovely to see, but it somehow looked just like many other great hotels and the girls were very glad that they were stopping at a small, really Swiss place.

They thought that way even more the next morning. Mrs. Merrill called them about eight o'clock. As Mary Jane opened her eyes and looked out the window she saw—whatever do you suppose? Where last night there had been nothing but clouds, now there was a great, gleaming mountain—its top entirely covered with snow. She could hardly believe her eyes, the sight was so startling and unexpected. Last night she had expected a mountain and there wasn't any. And now there it was— big as life!

She slipped on her dressing gown and ran out on the porch to see it the better. The reddish brown of the mountain, the snow white of the top, and the brilliant blue of the lake looked more like a picture in the Sunday newspaper than a real scene. It was no wonder that she thought at first that she must be dreaming.

"We're having our breakfast here on our own porch," said Mr. Merrill. He had just come in from an early morning walk and he looked as though he liked what he had seen.

"It's served in five minutes and if anyone is missing, I shall eat her strawberries, I promise you!"

But nobody was missing. Anyway, there was such a big bowl full of lovely berries that a person really had plenty by the time he had eaten his own share.

"Now then what do you do today?" asked Alice, as she finished the last bit of toast and honey.

"That's the question," said Mr. Merrill. "There's a boat leaving shortly for Geneva and I'm told it's a fine trip. It takes several hours but allows time for lunch and a quick drive round Geneva before returning. That would be fun. Or we can stay here a few hours and then go on to Interlaken today."

"Let's go on the boat," suggested Alice. "And of course we want to see Geneva because that's where people of many nations come. I've seen the picture of the League of Nations building and I'm sure I would know it if I saw it. And anyway, we don't want to ride on the train again right after yesterday, truly we don't."

That settled the question and with a bit of hurrying the Merrills made the boat just in time. The baggage was left at the hotel and with not a thing to bother about, the day's fun began.

THE CASTLE OF CHILLON

THE trip to Geneva was very jolly. The girls loved the boat ride with the views of mountains, small boats with twin sails of orange and red, the lovely city of Geneva with its great quay and lovely buildings. They had a very good luncheon on the boat and during their drive Alice *did* recognize the League of Nations building. And so the day was a complete success. After dinner in the evening, the Merrills window-shopped in Montreux and planned to stay past lunch time the next day, as they wanted to see the famous Castle of Chillon in the morning.

But the first thing that Mary Jane heard in the morning was thunder—great loud rumbles of thunder that shook the bed and startled her into instant awakefulness. She ran to the window to look out and to her amazement she found that the mountain was gone again. The great peak that had seemed so plain and so near yesterday was entirely gone and in its place was only a mass of dark clouds shot through with occasional lightning.

"It's a hide and seek game that old mountain plays," laughed the little girl as she called Alice to wake up and see, "but it can't fool me again, because now I know it's there all the time, back of the clouds!"

Breakfast was served on the little porch and the Merrills took time to linger because the storm was fun to watch. Suddenly rain descended in torrents and the few people on the streets scurried to shelter. Then, after the downpour, the clouds began to blow away and the sun shone so brilliantly that in fifteen minutes an outline of the mountain was beginning to show.

"Now we can go to the castle!" cried Alice, gleefully, when the first bit of sun sparkled across the porch. "Let's hurry so's to have plenty of time there!"

"You'd think she never saw a castle," laughed Mr. Merrill. But he got up from the table just the same and made ready to go.

"We haven't seen a Swiss castle," Alice reminded him. "And I want to be sure to see this one and get some pictures because we read about the Castle of Chillon in school. Everyone knows about it because there are so many colored pictures of it. You know, Mary Jane, the ones with the blue, blue lake, the white topped mountains, and the red-roofed castle with pointed peaks?"

"And boats with two sails and swans," asked Mary Jane, "the one we saw in the train coming down from Paris?"

"That's the one," agreed Alice. "Be sure you take your pocket book to buy pictures. I'm taking two rolls of films, for we don't want to miss getting a photograph."

They got aboard a small electric street-car and rode a short distance from town—right along the lake and the automobile road where they could see boats and travelers and small Swiss boys carrying loads on their backs. So far, while Switzerland had been interesting, there had been nothing as unusual about it as the girls had expected—except, perhaps, their hotel with its simple ways—so they were thrilled to see those boys with great baskets. They need not have wondered about seeing sights, as they found out quickly enough when they traveled further into the country.

At the castle, they got off the car and walked to the bridge where Alice took her first picture—and the last for a while too, as cameras were not allowed inside. But she got one of the rocky path, across the old rustic bridge that connected the small island of the castle with the mainland. That was something. Across the bridge they found a guide, paid their admissions, and began to see how wonderful the castle really was. The moat still had water flowing in it and the walls surrounded the little garden where roses bloomed on bushes more than a hundred years old. But inside were dungeons, torture rooms, warriors' halls and dark passages so many, so cold and stony and real that the girls shivered as they passed through. The hall of soldiers with its gaily painted walls was fun to see. In the old, old banquet hall there was a great stove that looked exactly like a pulpit in church, and in it food for scores was once cooked. This was interesting but for the most part the castle was gloomy and sad, though so mysterious, too, that the girls wouldn't have missed seeing it for anything.

"You know what I'd like to do," said Alice soberly, as they came up from the lowest dungeon. "When we get home, I'd like to visit a jail or a prison."

"Heavens!" exclaimed her mother, "haven't you seen enough today?"

"Yes," said Alice, "but this seems like a story book. It really is that, you know, Mother. What I'd like to see is a prison in our country today and see how much better it is—if it is better—than this old-time one."

"Good idea," approved her father. "I don't know just what we can do or see but we'll find out. There are a lot of bad prisons—disgraces to the states that keep them, but in the main you'll find them a lot better than this. You just wait and see."

Back at the bridge again the girls were very reluctant to leave. The dungeons were gloomy but the gardens with rose bushes and many other wonderful plants were lovely and even the dark prison seemed more story-bookish than real. A person would like to stay and make a story about the castle. Surely a little girl might have lived there sometime and had some strange adventures.

"Look at the swans," cried Mary Jane as she saw a flock of lovely swans swimming up toward the little covered bridge over the moat. "Let's get some bread and feed them as we fed the fish in Paris!"

There was no old woman handy to sell bread, but a little inquiring and a few coins produced two loaves which the girls broke into bits and tossed to the beautiful white birds.

"It's a shame I can't take a picture of this," cried Alice, "it would be so lovely and I'd have it for our English class at school."

"Alice!" Mary Jane's tone was quiet but so firm that Alice knew something was up.

"See that rock over there?"

Alice looked and saw a small flat rock, close by the water's edge but quite a bit beyond the wall that bordered the castle grounds.

"Yes," replied Alice, "it looks like a regular rock."

"It is, I 'spect," agreed Mary Jane, "but it's just outside the part where you can't use a camera."

"Mary Jane, you surely are a peach," cried Alice, excitedly. "I'll find Dad this minute and tell him I'm ready to go and we'll go out and watch for the street car. We'll get the camera on the way."

"And I," continued Mary Jane, plotting quickly, "will not notice when you go and maybe mother won't either. And I'll feed the swans till they think it's Thanksgiving in summer and you work your quickest so they don't get away."

Alice ran back to the entrance hall of the castle where her father and mother were still looking at pictures and documents.

"We're through looking around, Dadah,"

Alice remarked with all the casualness she could muster. "Mind if I go on ahead and get my camera and watch for the car?"

"No, run along, sister," Mr. Merrill said, not looking up. "We'll be out soon. It's high time we were getting off."

Alice had intended to tell him of her plan and ask him to go with her, but the guide was right there. Although she was sure there was no rule against taking pictures outside the castle grounds, still she didn't want to talk about it beforehand. So, thinking a minute, she decided to go on alone and take a chance. She strolled out to the gate, got her camera, crossed the little bridge without even a look at her small sister, and then hurried round the bend of the path, through the bushes and trees until she found the rock Mary Jane had pointed out.

It was smooth and flat and in two minutes Alice had taken four pictures of Mary Jane and the castle and the swans and everything. None too soon either, for as she snapped the last, the guide and her mother and father came from the castle. The guide playfully clapped his hands at the swans and away they fluttered, shrieking and screaming loudly.

Mary Jane tried to entice them back with the last bits of bread, but evidently they had had enough or else they didn't like to come back to where they had been frightened. For they sailed away, flapping their wings as they went. Mary Jane brushed the crumbs off her hands and frock and turned to follow her mother and father while Alice shut her camera carefully and climbed up from the rock. Had she known how very, very deep the water was right at the edge of that stone, perhaps she wouldn't have enjoyed her climb back as much. But she didn't know until her father told her on the way home. And so she climbed up very gaily without ever a thought of slipping.

Just as she was at the top, the clang of

the car bell sounded at the crossing and the car left without them. Alice ran as hard as she could through the trees, along the curving path, but the car was well down the road when she came in sight.

"Now, then," said Mr. Merrill when she caught up with them, "let's see what we had better do. Our train leaves at ten minutes to two this afternoon. It's now eleven and the next car is at eleven-thirty. I'm afraid no one is going to do any shopping in Montreux. Will you be very disappointed?"

"Not I," said Mrs. Merrill, comfortably. "I can find plenty to spend my money for some other place in Switzerland."

"Nor I," said Alice, "I've got my pictures and that's the most I care about. You know Interlaken was the place I intended to look for corals and I'm sure we can find pretty carvings there, too."

"But I wanted to get some post card pictures for my grandmother and for my collection," said Mary Jane. "What can I do about that?"

"We can go back to the entrance of the castle where they had lovely card pictures," said Mrs. Merrill, quickly. "I nearly got some anyway but I thought there might not be time."

So she and Mary Jane went back and bought two packages of six cards each—one for mailing and one for keeping. Then they joined Alice and Mr. Merrill out on the road.

"Let's walk along the road and let the car overtake us," he suggested. "We'll be riding on the train all afternoon and it will be fun to pretend we live here in Montreux and are walking back home. Let's go!"

So with a brisk, swinging step they set out along the road at the foot of the great mountain and made a good part of the way back to the town before the car came in sight. Then, in quick time, they were back at the hotel, with luncheon and packing to keep them busy till the train left.

The girls hated to leave their lovely rooms and their balcony for they were not likely to find another place as pretty. But train time came and off they went, ready for more exploring.

OVER THE MOUNTAINS

MARY JANE and Alice felt as though they were telling an old friend good-by when their porter-cook tucked away their bags on the train and gratefully accepted Mr. Merrill's generous tip. This hotel, the smallest of all they had visited, seemed so friendly and they had been so comfortable that they would like to stay longer. But they were getting used to the feeling of wanting to stay—and going right along in spite of that—so they said good-by very gaily and promised to come again to visit some other time.

"I haven't used any of my Swiss money," remarked Mary Jane, as she sat by the broad plate glass window. "And it's such pretty money."

"Don't forget that it's different from the

French money," said Mr. Merrill. "It sounds the same because there is a franc in each system. But the Swiss franc is a higher unit. I mean that it is worth more than the French, so don't get mixed and spend more than you have."

"Maybe I'd better pay you back for those post cards right now, mother," Mary Jane suggested. "Then I can see how it counts up." She spread out her few coins on her lap and separated the French from the Swiss. Then she paid her debt for the cards and counted again what was left. It was such absorbing business that she didn't notice when the train started; she couldn't be bothered with looking up till those coins were all sorted and back in the right compartments of her purse. Then she looked up to see where she was—and there wasn't anything out of the window! Just space! The houses and hotels were gone; the trees were gone. Not a thing was in sight except the snowcapped mountain across the lake.

The emptiness gave Mary Jane a funny flop right in the middle—it was so unexpected and so queer. She leaned up to the window and looked out and down. Their train was going *up the mountain* just as her father had said it would. The town of Montreux was already so far below that the roofs looked like a pattern in a quilt and the boats along the edge of the lake looked more the size of swans than real boats a person could ride in. It was all so amazing that Mary Jane didn't say a word till she had looked a while. Then suddenly, the train turned a bend in the track and Mary Jane's window looked out on trees and woods. The lake and town were way, way down on the *other* side of the car.

"Do you think we'll slide down or fall off or anything, Dadah?" she asked anxiously. "It seems awfully slippy to me."

"It seems slippy to anyone who lives in a place like Chicago where the highest hill isn't much higher than a viaduct," said her father, laughing. "But just remember that the Swiss railroads are as fine and safe as any in the world. And however high we are now, we'll probably go higher in a few minutes."

"Oh, we couldn't, Dadah!" exclaimed Mary Jane, incredulously. "We're almost as high as a mountain now!"

"It does seem so," laughed Mr. Merrill, "But you wait and see!"

"Mary Jane, look at these flowers!" interrupted Alice. She pulled Mary Jane to her window across the car. The train had turned again and was creeping slowly at this minute. The girls almost felt as though they could get out and pick the lovely pink, blue, white, and orange blossoms that grew so close to the track. It was more fun to watch the flowers than to look down the mountain, Mary Jane thought.

But soon she got more used to the feeling of height and could point down at the track where they had been without feeling queer

at all.   But she didn't get over the feeling
that she must not lean against the window
lest she tip the train over.   They seemed so
on the edge of the world!

After they had been traveling an hour
or so, Mary Jane wasn't afraid to move
about the train and she and Alice chatted
with two other girls from the United States
who were going to Interlaken, too.

"Are you going up the Jungfrau tomorrow?" asked Ellen, the older of the two.
"I want to go but mother and Sue don't like
to, so maybe I can't."

"We're not going to the top of anything,
not if it's higher than the train at this minute," said Mrs. Merrill, firmly.   "Mary
Jane and I don't like high places and we're
not going.   We've a nice trip of some sort
planned for tomorrow—I forget just what
it is, but you can be sure it's not to the top
of a mountain.   I told the travel bureau we
didn't want that."

"You and I should go with Dad," said

Alice, to Ellen, hopefully. "I like tops of things even though Mary Jane and Mother don't. Maybe he can take us."

"But we've our trip all planned for to-morrow," said Mrs. Merrill, "and what-ever it is I know it will be interesting. Then the next day we go on to Lucerne. But we're not over the pass yet today. I think you girls will feel quite high up in the world even though you don't go on the Jungfrau, so look out the windows and enjoy it while you're here."

Mary Jane had often read stories about a mountain pass but she hadn't really under-stood what it meant as she did at this min-ute. Here they were climbing back and forth, back and forth up the mountain, sometimes through tunnels but more often clinging close to the rock with a drop of goodness-knows-how-many feet right down from the track. Finally they got so high that they could see way down the lake toward Geneva—and still they climbed up.

Then suddenly there was a straight stretch and presto! Montreux, the lake, everything they had been looking at was gone. There was a *new* valley and a *new* mountain and new lakes—tiny sparkling ones. They had crossed a "pass!"

This valley was much more like the Switzerland the girls had expected to see—naturally, because it was more isolated than Montreux. The houses were of wood—browned with age. The roofs stuck out at the gables and many a house had small balconies just like the doll Swiss village Mary Jane once saw in a store at Christmas time. She forgot to be afraid of the mountain and of falling and stood up at the window the better to see down the valley.

"Wouldn't it be fun to live in a house like that?" she exclaimed as they spied a lovely place half way down the mountain. It was built on posts and under the house were great piles of wood—plenty to keep the family in firewood for the long, cold winter. There were stairways up the outside of the house, at each end, and boxes of gay flowers at all the windows.

"It looks just like a doll house!" exclaimed Alice, in delight. "I can't believe that it's real and that people live in it and keep house and everything."

"But they certainly do," said her father. "In the winter time they very much live in it, for they are often snow-bound for days at a time. That's when the men and boys do the carving you will see and the women and girls make the lace and embroider the linen you have heard about. Just imagine this valley all piled up with snow and ice and then think how snug such a house would be. Look! There's an old one with stones on the roof to keep the wind from blowing it off! Switzerland has been so prosperous of late that many new roofs have been put on in place of the old ones. So look hard when you see stones—that means a really old roof—the kind you have seen in pictures."

All the time they had been looking, the train had been creeping down the mountain —down and down and down; just as it had gone up on the other side. But this time the girls were more used to it and Mary Jane didn't find it frightening at all, though it still made her feel queer when she thought of it. Fortunately, they were so busy watching for roofs, seeing flower-trimmed houses and other sights that she didn't often stop to think.

In each village there was a church with a steeple and on the mountain-sides, sheep grazed and shepherds cared for them while around the farm-houses the girls could see people coming and going about their business in a most every-day sort of fashion. Otherwise it would almost have seemed as though the valley was a picture—not a place that was real.

Up from the valley they climbed again, up and up and at the very top of this pass they stopped to change engines. The girls got out, along with many other passengers and some bought cups of hot chocolate at a small house close to the track.

"Let's get some milk chocolate to eat on the train," suggested Alice, "maybe we wouldn't have time to drink a cup of chocolate because it looks awfully hot."

"There's some just like the ones we buy at home!" exclaimed Mary Jane, in great surprise, as she pointed to a pile of cakes of chocolate that looked very familiar. "I didn't suppose we could get American chocolate up here on the mountain!"

"You're saying it the behind side around," laughed her mother. "We get Swiss chocolate at home. The very best milk chocolate is made right here in Switzerland and sent to America—no wonder it looks natural."

They bought several bars and the girls found it delicious—fresh and sweet and oh, so good.

As their train crawled down from this last pass, clouds covered the sky and the Merrills couldn't see the valley. They could only get glimpses of houses near the track and those were small and far, far between. But there was plenty to see none the less—the rocks, the wonderfully laid, curving track, trees and clouds. They went through a drizzle of rain and then, just a few minutes before they were due at Interlaken, the sun struggled out and the clouds broke away.

"We'll not need our umbrellas after all," said Alice, strapping hers back onto her suitcase. "Do you suppose we can walk to our hotel here, Dad, or is it a long way?" Of course her father didn't know, but the Boston lady they had been chatting with told them it was quite a journey—that is, too long to walk with bags.

When they got to the station they discovered interesting looking buses and they quickly found places in one marked, "Savoy Hotel" and soon were clattering down the street to that hotel.

It seemed very funny to be on the ground again and have the mountains up against the sky where they belonged. After they were shown to their rooms Mary Jane said, "We're not one bit mussed up Alice, that train was so clean. Let's walk down the hall to that upstairs porch and look around before we dress for dinner."

Alice, with a glance at her watch, agreed that there was plenty of time, so they tip-toed down the hall and out onto a large un-roofed balcony at the end. The sun was shining brilliantly now and the clouds of the afternoon were almost gone. Mary Jane looked north across the green at the village, the hotels, the parks and the people strolling along. Then she looked south— and there, high, so high it seemed to go al-most to the middle of the sky, was a moun-tain. And down from the top of the mountain was a river of ice that gleamed white and blue as the sun shone on it.

"It's a glacier!" exclaimed the two girls in an awe-struck whisper.

"It's a *real* glacier!" cried Mary Jane.

"It's the Jungfrau!" added Alice, delighted that she could recognize it from the pictures she had seen.

"Let's tell mother!" cried Mary Jane, and, forgetting all about being a quiet little lady, she ran pell mell down the hall to fetch her mother.

CORALS AND CARVINGS

ALICE had felt very knowing about Switzerland. Hadn't she seen pictures—hundreds of them? Didn't she know about mountains and glaciers and valleys and all such? Of course any little girl who is nearly ready for high school knows a lot about such things. But *seeing* them— that was different. And as for Mary Jane, she didn't pretend to know much about strange countries because she hadn't studied geography very far yet and she was thrilled to see anything as wonderful as that glacier looked when the sun shone on it. If she hadn't known what it was, she'd have guessed it was something uncommon—a person could tell that, even though she wasn't very old.

Mr. and Mrs. Merrill came to see it and

they all lingered till a gong in the hall reminded them that dinner would be served
soon.

"It's been here hundreds of years," re-
marked Alice as the gong sounded, "and
I'm guessing it will still be there tomorrow.
And I'm *not* guessing about something else
—I *know* that I'm hungry!"

After dinner there was still a little twi-
light, so Mary Jane suggested a walk.
"Maybe we can see some stores and buy
some souvenirs," she added, hopefully.

"Not this time of evening," said Alice.
"Don't you remember that every thing was
shut at Montreux? But we can window-
shop—that's almost as much fun. And it
will help us to decide what we want and
where to get it tomorrow."

The valley that was Interlaken had a
long, narrow strip of park in the middle. On
either side of the park were great hotels—
perhaps the bigger ones were on the north
side but some of the newer ones were on the

south where the Merrills were staying. All
along the street on the north side of the park
were shops—pretty little one-story shops
packed full of interesting and lovely things.
The girls ran from one side of the road to
the other looking at windows and it wasn't
till they had been by half a dozen that they
even noticed that the stores were open and
doing a thriving business with the tourists.

"We can buy anything we like," exclaimed Mary Jane, delightedly, when she
noticed that a store which had a window
full of lovely carved ivory was open.

"You mean, you can buy if you have the
money," teased her father. "That's as important in Interlaken as in Chicago, I
fancy."

Mary Jane made a little grimace at him
and then pointed out a little ivory dog she
had been admiring.

"It's only a little dog, Dadah," she
showed him. "Wouldn't you think I could
buy it?"

"Only one way to tell," he replied. "Ask the price. It's your business, so you ask them."

Remembering her embarrassment in Paris at shops where only French was spoken she hesitated. But the little dog was very much to her liking so she finally summed up courage and went inside. She needn't have been timid for the store-keeper was most kind and friendly. He followed her to the window and saw just which dog she wanted. Then in the best of English, he told her the price was twenty francs and showed her a whole tableful of carved dogs, inside the store. There were running dogs and standing dogs, sitting dogs and dogs lying down; there were shaggy dogs and short haired dogs—though many more shaggy ones than the others. In fact, most of them looked like the St. Bernard dogs so famous in mountain stories.

"But twenty francs!" Mary Jane tried to compute. If it was French francs that would be simple enough for she knew twenty francs were worth less than one United States dollar. But Swiss money was different and she couldn't feel sure. If only a person could spread out the money and count!

"Figure about five francs to each dollar, Mary Jane," whispered Mrs. Merrill, seeing Mary Jane's distress. "That may not be exact but it's near enough so you can tell whether you can afford to get what you want."

"Five francs to a dollar—twenty francs," Mary Jane whispered it over to herself. "Why! That's *four* dollars for just one little dog!" she exclaimed in amazement. "I couldn't ever spend so much! Why does it cost *that?* It's such a *little* dog!"

"Little, yes, miss," said the storekeeper, quickly. "But see the carving! For days a man works to make the fine carving of the hair, the eyes, the feet, the ears. Twenty francs are very little for such fine carving."

Indeed, Mary Jane thought so, too, as she studied the lovely little piece. But alas! Her thinking that didn't put another franc in her pocket-book so she reluctantly put the dog down and went out without it. Maybe —but no, she'd think it over before spending that much. As soon as she got back to her room she'd count out all her money and see. Maybe the dog would still be there to-morrow. At least she could hope it would be.

The next store had lovely corals and Alice was soon busy looking at various strings.

"You know, Dadah," she planned, quickly, "I think I'll spend my birthday money for some corals. When I got my birthday check, I thought it was funny to have money instead of a present, but now I think it's wonderful. See these?" she held up a string of lovely, pale pink corals. "These cost just the amount of my birthday money and I couldn't ever find any I'd like better."

"Slip them over your head," suggested the storekeeper, kindly. "Here is a mirror. See the length? A little short, perhaps, for miss. Maybe this would be better."

He dropped another string, quite a bit longer, over Alice's head. And while she was admiring those and wondering which of the two was the best length, he hunted up a third one and tried that one, too.

Alice studied the mirror, she asked advice and finally decided to buy the third string which was between the other two in length. She took it off and laid it on the counter to be wrapped. Then reluctantly she took off the other—it was so rosy and lovely—but really too long to look right, she thought.

In a very business-like fashion she counted out the Swiss coins, took her parcel and the Merrills went on. Mrs. Merrill wanted to look at laces and embroideries and there were many interesting shops they wanted to see.

They strolled past a couple of large

hotels, more shops and were just turning into an embroidery shop when someone grabbed Mary Jane from the back, put hands firmly over her eyes and in a high, disguised voice said, "Guess who!"

Mary Jane quickly thought of all the people who might be in Interlaken—the two girls they had talked with on the train that day; someone from the boat maybe—but those people weren't old enough friends to make a person guess like that! Then she remembered—"Doris Dana!" she exclaimed, quickly, as she grabbed down the hands and whirled around.

"Pooh! You shouldn't have guessed!" laughed Doris, pleased nevertheless to be welcomed. "We weren't coming till tomorrow and I was sure you wouldn't know! Now let's walk ahead and look at windows."

As Mrs. Merrill wanted to linger at the linen shop, it was decided that the three girls should walk on as far as the street was

wide and turn back when it narrowed. Mrs.
Dana was shopping, too, and Doris had left
her when she spied Mary Jane through a
window, so they greeted her and then
started on their walk.

There was so much to see that it took
them a long time to go a block. In front
of the linen shop pretty girls in gay peasant
costumes sat at their embroidery frames putting initials on handkerchiefs for tourists'
orders; windows were full to overflowing
with all sorts of lovely native goods—from
carvings to chocolates, so the three girls
looked and chattered and had a beautiful
time until suddenly Doris remarked,
"You've a lovely string of coral, Alice.
Where did you buy it?"

Alice held her precious box tightly and
replied, "Back at the shop just before the
big hotel. It's a fine shop, too. And I'll
show you my corals as soon as we get to our
rooms."

"But I can see them now," said Doris, surprisingly. "They're lovely."

Mary Jane looked at Doris in amazement. How could she see Alice's corals when they were packed away with tissue paper and wrappings in a box in Alice's hand? Then she looked at Alice to see what she made of the puzzle. And what do you suppose she saw? You've guessed? Yes.

There was that third string of corals around Alice's neck—and the store where it belonged was blocks and blocks away. What would that nice storekeeper think? Would they be arrested for stealing? How should they return it? Mingled with the crowd here and there they had spied pleasant-looking, gaily uniformed officers. Suppose one of them had been told to "watch for the American girl who had taken the corals away?" Would they realize that it was just a careless mistake? Mary Jane's face burned with embarrassment, and from the way Alice looked it was plain she was having the same painful thoughts.

"I'll tell you what we should do," said Alice, after a few seconds thought. "I think we should act just as though nothing had happened. Only—we should turn around at once and go straight for the shop where this belongs. Then if any one finds us, we are at least going in the right direction. Let's not run or make any commotion—just walk as quickly as we can."

That seemed a good idea, so the girls started immediately. Never had they felt so uncomfortably conspicuous. It seemed as though *everyone* looked at that necklace and Mary Jane had to press her lips together tightly to keep from saying, "She's taking it back! She's taking it back now!"

As they passed the shop where they had left Mrs. Merrill, they looked in but couldn't see either their father or mother— how could they when both had just stepped into a back room to select some samples of monograming? But Alice thought it was more important to get the necklace back than to wait for parents so the three girls hurried on.

When they reached the coral shop Alice felt ashamed to go in. The store-keeper had been so very kind—but what would he think? But there was nothing else to do, so in she had to go.

But it wasn't hard at all. He came toward her smiling and said, pleasantly, "Oh, did you find it?" Just that way as though it was a nice little joke between friends.

"I didn't mean to take it," began Alice, miserably, but he waved her words aside and said, "I didn't notice either till just as you were outside. Then I didn't bother because I knew you would discover it sometime and would bring it back."

"You didn't think I would take it?" asked Alice, happily.

"I *knew* you wouldn't," he replied firmly.

"I knew it was perfectly safe. I can tell my people; I know who to trust." And he helped Alice take it off and smiled in friendly fashion as the girls left.

"Isn't he the nicest man who ever kept a store!" exclaimed Mary Jane, gleefully, once they were again on the walk.

"And isn't Switzerland the best country!" cried Alice, nearly bursting with relief. "He didn't seem to even suspect my taking that—and just as *nice* to us!

"Just you wait till we find Dadah! Haven't we a tale to tell, though?"

And off they hurried back to the linen shop.

IN THE LAUTERBRUNNEN
VALLEY

MARY JANE and her mother stood at the porter's desk in the lobby of the Savoy early in the morning of the next day. They had happened to be ready for breakfast ahead of the others and had agreed to pick up the tickets for their outing-tickets that had been ordered in advance for them by the travel bureau.

"But these seem to say the Jungfrau trip," objected Mrs. Merrill, as she tried to decipher the French and German with which they were inscribed. "And we especially said that we wanted a nice trip but *not* a high one."

The porter looked surprised. "But madam," he said, in his excellent English —all Swiss hotel porters seemed to speak

77

beautiful English—"nice trips in Switzerland are always high. Our mountains are our country. You will like this trip I know. It is easy and comfortable. Even the little lady here cannot help enjoy it." Mary Jane looked a bit dubious. The top of the Jungfrau seemed much too cold and high to be pleasant—except as a picture way off. But he went right on.

"The train is very comfortable. Everyone goes. And anyway, the tickets are bought." There seemed nothing to answer to that for there the tickets were, bought and paid for.

"Let's go, mother," suggested Mary Jane. "We haven't fallen off any train yet. We won't mind it nearly as much as we did at first. And look at the long tickets! So many places we can go! Let's do it, mother!"

"If you take the early train you can stop off at Lauterbrunnen," suggested the porter. "An hour's stay there between trains is very interesting. You can see the falls and the little lady can see the boys and girls in the valley. Very nice houses and little villages. I think you would like it."

The plan sounded fine to Mary Jane so she dashed back up the stairs to tell Alice and her father to hurry as there were only fifty minutes till the train left—and the station was at the opposite end of the village from where they had arrived and was quite a drive away. But even though they must hurry, Mrs. Merrill took time to send a message to Ellen telling her of their plan for the day and inviting her to meet them on the train if she cared to. And that's just what she did. They found her eagerly awaiting them when they arrived at the station.

"It's very good of you to take Ellen," said her mother, appreciatively.

"We're glad to have her company," said Mrs. Merrill, "and she is lucky to be able to get a ticket. They tell me the next train

is full. The journey must be safe enough
if so many go. So don't be anxious, we'll
try to take good care of her."

The Merrills found by the chatting of
people around them that others were stopping off at Lauterbrunnen, too. The day
was delightful—sunny and warm and just
right for sight-seeing. As the little train
wound around the valley the girls found
much to see—mountains, rivers, glaciers,
forests, and then, when they reached the
Lauterbrunnen valley itself, interesting
looking people. There was a tiny little station and in the front three pretty girls in
native dress sat on little stools embroidering
diligently.

"I'd like to sew with a hoop like that,"
said Mary Jane, admiringly. The dainty
work was held on a round hoop of wood
which was clamped to an upright post. The
girl sat on a three-legged stool—like an
old fashioned milking stool of colonial
times and her bright eyes didn't seem one bit

bothered by the tiny, tiny stitches she was taking.

"Just imagine people sitting embroidering at a station in Chicago—or any place at home," laughed Alice. "She looks so pretty."

"And she certainly is good for business," added Mr. Merrill, "see the ladies from our train who are giving orders or making purchases. The Swiss people have good sense in their selling, you can see that. And as they are industrious and skilful workers as well, you can understand why their small country is so prosperous."

Just beyond the station were some waiting busses and the drivers called for passengers to go to the falls. One middle-sized bus quite took Mary Jane's fancy and she asked to ride in it. There were seats for three—several of them, and the girls chose the back seat for themselves. Mr. and Mrs. Merrill sat with the driver and other tourists filled the rows in between.

"Now hold on tightly," cautioned Mrs. Merrill, as she saw the girls settle themselves and prepared to climb into the place she had chosen, "because we can't see you from the front."

The girls laughingly promised to hold on very tightly and in another minute the bus started.

They went down a pretty little road that became more and more untraveled-looking as it got farther from the station. The great mountains rose up high on either side and the girls could see grazing cattle and pretty little houses as well as forests and people and flowers and goats and so many sights that each girl "oh"-ed and exclaimed without even waiting to see what the other girl was talking about. The road dwindled into a wide path and the bus jolted from one side to the other till the girls really did have to hold tightly to keep from falling. But they thought it was fun—much more fun than a smooth, paved road.

As they crossed a tiny creek someone suggested that it was a fine place for pictures so the obliging driver stopped. The girls promptly got down and while Ellen and Alice and the others who wanted pictures talked about backgrounds and focuses, Mary Jane wandered along the side of the road. There, back of a big tree was a small boy, resting. On his back was strapped a great basket—oh, a basket much, much bigger than a bushel basket—and what do you suppose it had in it? Grass. Freshly cut grass, looking almost like the grass Mary Jane often played with when her father used to cut their lawn before they moved to their Chicago home. But this grass was longer, though still fresh and green.

What in the world would a boy be doing with all that grass? Mary Jane wondered so hard that she forgot about language and asked him. But though he shyly said two or three words, she couldn't make out what he meant. He pointed up the mountain path

behind her to a small ridge where a half
dozen cows were grazing and made motions
which said very plainly that he was taking
it up for them to eat. It almost made Mary
Jane tired to think about carrying such a
load so far, but the boy seemed not to mind.
She stood there looking at him, wishing
there were words to talk because there was
a lot she would have liked to say when suddenly he jumped and grabbed at her frantically. At the same instant Alice's voice
back at the road shouted, "Look out, Mary
Jane! RUN!" But neither warning was
in time, for around the side of a clump of
bushes, behind Mary Jane's back, charged a
goat so fast and so hard that he seemed to
appear from nowhere. Before Mary Jane
suspected that she was in danger she was
tossed lightly to one side of the bushes and
the angry goat was on his way to further
mischief.

In a daze she sat up and rubbed her hurt
elbow and her head.

"Look out Mary Jane! Run!"

"Mary Jane! Mary Jane, dear, are you hurt?" cried Alice dropping her camera and running to her sister. She was the first to reach Mary Jane and Ellen was close behind. The grown-ups back at the coach, had heard the commotion, but as Mary Jane was out of sight around the clump of bushes, they didn't know anything had happened to her until Alice called. Then they came hurrying to see.

Very fortunately the grass-boy, by his effort to get Mary Jane out of the goat's way, had been able to move her enough to save the worst of the shock. The creature hit her on the side instead of head-on, as he otherwise would have done. No telling how bad an injury there might have been had the boy not tried to save her. Outside some bruises, she seemed unhurt. So by the time her parents arrived she was up and trying to laugh bravely even though she was still too shaky to do it very successfully.

The passengers on the bus were not the

only ones who heard the screams and came hurrying. A good Swiss matron from the house close by came out to see what had happened and when she found a little girl had been knocked over—and by one of the woman's own goats, too, she was anxious to do something to make amends. She chattered excitedly with the driver and then after she had been assured that there was no real injury and no hard feelings—only a bumped head and elbow, she smiled and invited Mary Jane to come to the house for a drink of milk. Of course, Mary Jane, not understanding German, didn't know what she was being invited to do, but she could tell by the woman's smiles and gestures that she was planning something friendly.

"She's wanting you to go to the house and have a drink of milk," one of the passengers explained. "Why don't you? It would be fun and you will feel better."

"But is there time?" asked Mrs. Merrill.

"Or perhaps there is a later bus we could take," suggested Mr. Merrill.

"There is plenty of time, sir," the driver assured him. "We will wait for the little lady. She is very brave and we will want her to be comfortable."

So Mary Jane, followed by Alice and Ellen, her father and mother, and several of the passengers, walked up the path to the nearby house, the kind Swiss mother running excitedly ahead and shouting directions as she ran.

Childish heads peeped out of windows, chickens and ducks ran scampering and a few goats in the yards (no doubt timid relations of the one who had caused all the trouble) turned and stared in surprise at the strange happenings in the usually quiet valley.

Mary Jane followed the mother around to the back where an outside stairway ascended to the second floor and made a sort of porch over the doorway. There on a bench was a great bowl of milk, covered with a cloth and wooden board. With a dipper the woman dipped milk and poured it into a beautifully carved wooden cup, which she quickly brought from inside the house. She handed this to Mary Jane with a curtsey—not so easy a thing to do, for she was heavy and breathless from hurrying. Then she went again into the house and returned with an apronful of cups of various kinds. These she filled with milk and gave them first to the girls and then to the others. The milk was warmish and odd tasting. Mary Jane didn't know whether she could drink it or not, but fortunately one of the travelers, who evidently had been in Switzerland enough to know something about it, explained that the milk was goat's milk and no doubt very fresh and good. So she drank it all and, after the first taste, found it very nice.

"Let me pay for our milk," said Mr. Merrill, as he returned his cup. The woman couldn't understand his words but she saw him take out his pocket-book and she shook her head vigorously.

"No, no!" she exclaimed, "No, no, no!"

"Then let us buy something," suggested the lady who spoke German. That idea pleased the woman very much. With a look of delight she hurried again into the house and returned with some lovely lace still on a frame, and some narrower lace which she had hastily gathered up.

In a moment the lace was sold and she went back into the house again, returning this time with a tiny wooden boy, beautifully carved and tinted. On his back was a basket of grass—he was modeled exactly like the boy who had tried to befriend Mary Jane and who now hung back on the edge of the crowd too interested in all that was going on to go away about his work.

"Oh, Dadah, this is just what I want!"

cried Mary Jane, happily. "It's just the right size and everything. Do let's get it! Do you suppose it costs too much!"

"I don't suppose it does," he answered, "but whatever it costs, I'll get it for you as a souvenir of our visit to this farm-house. It isn't every little girl who comes a-touring Switzerland and gets knocked down by a goat and then goes visiting in a real Swiss farm-house. I know that!" But when the woman found that Mary Jane wanted the carving, she wouldn't take money for it. Instead she handed it to her with a gesture that said as plainly as words she was welcome to it.

Then, as she went into the house, she motioned Mary Jane to come to the door. Inside was a large room, quite bare (according to Mary Jane's ideas). There was a table covered with a red cloth, a few stools and one chair. And over in the corner was a cradle with a real baby as plump and rosy as a Christmas doll. From the pile of work by the cradle, she selected a handkerchief which she gave the little girl. Mary Jane would have liked to stay a long time—long enough to learn how to talk to the little girl about her lace-making and the baby sister she was busily rocking. But instead the bus-driver's horn, blowing loudly, called her back to the door. With a hearty "thank you," which the Swiss family must have understood, the Merrills left hurriedly. The two pictures of the house and family which Alice had taken quickly after running back for her camera while Mary Jane was indoors, the handkerchief and the little carved boy would be prized souvenirs of their only call at a real Swiss house.

As they hurried down the path to the road a toothless grandmother joined the mother and children in waving good-by and in saying words that meant "Good luck! Good journey!"

LUNCHEON AT SCHEIDEGG

AFTER the delay, the coach hurried along as fast as the horses dared pull it over the stony roads till they arrived at the Trummelbach Falls down the valley. Mary Jane had been watching as they rode along, for she thought there might be something like Niagara Falls. Over the noise of the clattering coach she began to hear a roar that got louder and louder as they went down the narrowing valley. Suddenly the driver crossed a small bridge, turned quickly to the right and stopped so close up against the side of the mountain that it seemed to stand right up—almost on top of the people.

"Better get out and walk up closer," he shouted over the roar.

Directly in front of the coach was a tossing, tumbling little stream. High up the mountain side was a cloud of white spray from which tumbled a narrow, swift-flowing mass of white. That was the falls. The passengers got out and walked across a small foot-bridge and up the path right under the falls. It was all wet and the air was filled with spray and the roar of the water was so great a person had to shout and make gestures to be understood.

Mary Jane could see that the falls were beautiful. The water dropped down from high up the mountain; then it got lost *in* the mountain, then came out a great hole and dashed down to the little stream at the bottom. There wasn't a doubt but that it was very wonderful and beautiful. But the noise and the rushing didn't seem very pleasant—perhaps because of her bumped head—so she was glad when the driver called "All a-board!" They had to hurry back to the train.

This mountain train had coaches more like street-cars than like cars on a regular train. Some of the seats were open like old-fashioned summer street cars—the seats running all the way across and no wall— only an iron handle at the end. When she got on board at Interlaken, Mary Jane had carefully avoided that open seat, because, remembering the high mountains coming from Montreux, she didn't want to sit on an edge. But the journey from Interlaken to Lauterbrunnen had been very comfortable and entirely in the valley. So this time she picked out a seat vacated by people who got off as the Merrills got on, and she sat right on the edge where she could see the girls who were embroidering in front of the station, and grin at them till the train pulled out.

But alas for plans! No sooner had the train pulled away from the station and crossed the little valley than it began to go up. Up this way a bit, then around a high curve and up some more. At first Mary Jane looked across the valley at the houses and farms and paid no attention to anything close by. But soon they were so high that a person just couldn't ignore the big empty space outside the car.

"Will you change places with me, Alice?" asked Mary Jane, in a meek little voice— quite different from the gay manner in which she had taken the end seat a few minutes before.

"Surely I will, Pussy," replied Alice, good-naturedly. "You sit next to me, here. But don't you be bothered by going up. See how steadily the train rides along. Look ahead and see how smooth and firm the track is. And look at those workmen. Dadah says they are working on the track all the time, keeping it in perfect condition so that it will be safe for travelers. Now don't you be afraid."

Mary Jane felt very comforted; Alice certainly knew just the right words to say to help a person. Holding tightly to Alice with one hand and the back of the seat with the other, Mary Jane crawled over her sister and took the next seat. Ellen, who was no more bothered by height than Alice, sat on the end seat just opposite. Sometimes the train came to a place where there was ground on both sides. Then it would turn and twist and climb right up the mountain on a cog-wheel track. They seemed to be traveling along on a narrow shelf on the side of the mountain.

They passed tiny villages and great hotels. Mary Jane spelled out the long names on the signs while the passengers got off and on but she couldn't say them, they were too long and strange for her to pronounce. Everyone seemed to be having a jolly time. Lots of folks were in sports clothes; most of them wore very heavy shoes and many carried small bags over the shoulders, showing that they were on tramping tours and were not bothered with trunks or luggage. People on the train and at the tiny stations chattered in English and Ger-

man and French—Mary Jane could tell by
the sounds which the languages were even
though she couldn't understand what was
said.

Finally the train got so high, high up
that she could see miles and miles down or
across the valley. They passed by many
small shacks and flocks of goats and herds
of cattle—not great numbers as there might
have been at home, but a few at a place
guarded over by a man or boy who lived in
the little shack. Mary Jane remembered
the stories she had been told of the Swiss
boys who leave their homes at the beginning
of summer and take the cattle high up on
the mountains where they can get fine food
for grazing. And there they stay, all summer, sometimes in sight of their homes down
in the valley, but not returning or having
any company or fun till the summer is over,
the cows are fat and healthy, and the little
house packed full of cheese made from the
rich milk.

It had been interesting enough to hear all about that but it was a lot more fun to see it with her own eyes, you may be sure.

And the flowers! So many of them and so gay and bright! Forget-me-nots almost (not quite, of course) as big as pansies, buttercups, violets, and blue bells nodding in the sun and scores of others the names of which the girls did not know. Sometimes the flowers were so close to the train that it seemed as though a person might jump out and pick a few, for the train went by so closely. But fortunately no one tried. If the train *did* go slowly, it went steadily along and a person wouldn't care to be left behind half way up the mountain.

"There's a flower like those we saw carved in ivory," said Mary Jane, as she spied her first real edelweiss growing on a rock, quite away from the other flowers. "I'd like one of those for my scrap book!" she exclaimed, admiringly.

"I'm afraid you can't get one," said her

father from the seat behind her, "for you see, the train moves right along. But I'll tell you what you can do. When we get back to Interlaken tonight you can buy an ivory edelweiss to wear as a pin. That won't fade and change. And now that you've really seen the flower, you can tell how very beautifully and truly they are reproduced in carvings."

Mary Jane thought that would be a good plan but there was no time now to talk about how much it would cost or where was a good place to buy it, for there was too much she wanted to see. They were going straight up the mountain again and the chill air, the smaller trees, and the many great bare rocks showed that they were now very high.

Soon they swung around to a station a little larger than the rest. A sign told them that they had arrived in Scheidegg—the end of that part of their trip. On the next track was a waiting train and many of their fel-

low passengers climbed onto it at once; but
Mr. Merrill had decided that they would
get their luncheon in Scheidegg and go up
the Jungfrau on the next train, an hour
later.

So they took their time getting away from
the station and strolled over to the great
four-story frame hotel nearby. Mary Jane
looked around, but she was too hungry and
chilly to be much interested in more sights.
The tables spread with red and white
checked cloths and the waiters coming and
going from the hotel porch were what caught
her eye.

"Let's have our luncheon now," she
urged, "and then look around. And let's
have it hot."

"I was just wondering about eating inside
or out," said Mrs. Merrill, as she stepped
across the porch and looked in at the cosy,
long hall made warm by three great fire-
places.

"Oh, let's eat on the porch," said Alice.

"We can eat indoors anywhere. But we can't always see a mountain with snow on the top."

That seemed a good argument, especially as they found a table in the sunshine where they could get served at once.

"What are you going to have, Dadah?" asked Mary Jane as she looked at her long card covered entirely with strange words, not one of which was in English so she could read it.

"Um-m-m—I hardly know yet," he replied, scanning his card much as Mary had hers. "We want something hot and quick and——"

"Maybe a good thick soup?" suggested the waiter in the usual good English.

"Just the thing," approved Mr. Merrill, much relieved. "Bring the best you've got and plenty of it. Then we'll see what else we want."

The waiter hurried briskly away, and as he left, Mary Jane spied the train leaving the station. "Now let's watch," she said, "and see it go up the mountain."

But that train didn't go up the mountain. It went across the meadow all gay with flowers, across the road where some people were walking, over to the side of the mountain—and then—presto! it disappeared right *into* the mountain itself. That was the last of it—track, poles, train—all stopped at the small dark hole on the side of the mountain.

Of course Mary Jane had seen tunnels and on the two train trips since leaving Paris, she had been through several. But never before had she seen a train go head on into a hole when there wasn't some apparent place for it to come out. The sight made her feel very queer.

Fortunately the next minute the waiter set before her a great bowl of steaming hot soup. It was thick and creamy and floating on the top were toasted bits of cracker, creamy with cheese. Best of all, the steam rising from it showed that it was good and hot. For a fleeting second Mary Jane thought of the Christmas poem which says, "He spake not a word but went straight to his work"—for she began eating without a word of talk and she ate right through that whole big bowlful of soup before she said anything.

"There now!" she finally exclaimed when she had nearly taken the bottom off the dish in her effort to get all the goodness, "I feel better. I guess what was the matter with me wasn't the goat or the mountains. It was my being hungry."

"But more is coming," Alice reminded her," you mustn't be full too soon!"

"Me full with just a bowl of soup?" exclaimed Mary Jane, disgustedly. "I'm surprised at you, Alice! I've only begun!"

But by the time dessert arrived she had lost interest in eating, for the meat and vegetables were all so good. She only sampled the pudding and as the others ate she watched the mountain where the train had gone in. That was how it happened that soon she saw a train come *out* of the tunnel just as the other had gone in. It hurried along across the meadows, along the road in front of the hotel and came to a stop at the station half a block away.

"There's the train again," cried Mary Jane, after she spied it.

"I doubt if that's the one. It's a long trip to the top," said her father. "But at least, it's one just like it. And it's the one we should take if we are to have any time on the top. How soon does it leave?" he asked the waiter.

"In about ten or twelve minutes, sir," was the reply.

So the Merrills hastily gathered up belongings and hurried over to board the train. They were none soo soon either, for the arrival of another train from Interlaken brought many travelers and every seat was filled when the whistle of the guard started

them off.   Mary Jane had a window seat,
and, as they got under way, she looked
across to the tunnel entrance where they
would soon disappear.   What would it be
like?   Would it be fun?   She wondered.

THE TOP OF THE WORLD

THE open meadow at Scheidegg had the loveliest flowers the girls had yet seen. Great forget-me-nots as blue as the sky overhead; buttercups as golden as the sun and such a profusion of blossoms that a person would have hard work to walk across without stepping on them. Alice and Ellen exclaimed and exclaimed till they were nearly breathless. But Mary Jane was so busy expecting the entrance to the tunnel and blinking ready for the coming darkness, that she hardly saw a thing.

Then, when they did get to the tunnel the lights in the car (which she had not noticed before because of the sunshine) kept total darkness away so it was not as dark as she had expected.

But it was dark enough, goodness knows!

And cold. And damp. Great drops of dampness clung to the walls and the windows got steamy and queer.

The train didn't go very rapidly. It went heavily with now and then a rattle of the cogs and the gleam of a red light. Mary Jane didn't say anything. She tried at first, but everyone on the train was so quiet that her words sounded like a yell and she didn't try again. She pushed up close to Alice and watched carefully out of the window.

After a while the train stopped and people gaily climbed out. Mary Jane wondered if this was the top. Surely they hadn't been an hour! And indeed, she was right, they hadn't been much more than a quarter of an hour but they had arrived at the first of the three stops.

The Merrills got out, and found that they were to look out through a great glass window set in the rock at the side of the track. They could see masses of snow and mountains, mountains and more mountains, look-

ing like a picture framed by rock. The
flowers and sunshine were all gone; all she
could see was clouds and snow. But of
course it was beautiful and wonderful to
see. So she looked carefully and then, like
the others, climbed back into the car. Again
they were off. Three times they stopped
and got out to look from these great windows, but at the last two they saw very
little as a snow storm had set in and all they
could see was fast falling flakes. It seemed
like a strange dream to leave so many
flowers and summer sights and in less than
an hour to be in a snow storm.

After the third stop the train pulled and
creaked. Mary Jane could tell by the feel
of it and by the way the seat tilted that
they were climbing very steeply. But by
this time the people were used to it and
the darkness and chattered gaily. It seemed
more fun than when the tunnel began.
Soon the guard called "Jungfraujoch!"
Mary Jane recognized that word and knew

that they had come to the end of their journey.

Along with the others they left the train and went into the inn. There was a large, comfortable living room with rows of windows on one side and two doors leading to a narrow porch outside. The living room was furnished with tables and chairs and at one end was a counter where pictures, postcards, candies, and other supplies popular with travelers were displayed.

Alice and Ellen hurried to the nearest door and went out on the porch, a sort of balcony. Mary Jane looked out of the windows and then decided it was silly not to go with the others so she went out too, although the falling snow and the peaks topped with ice and snow warned her that she would be cold.

She went out in time to see Alice leaning over the side to look down, down—oh, a person couldn't tell how many thousands of feet down into ice and snow. As they watched, the snow suddenly stopped and there was a gleam of sun through the clouds. The girls could see small figures roped together climbing along a glacier far off on one side and other figures also tied together climbing rocks on another side.

"Now let's see if we can go up to the top," said Alice after she had looked carefully at the scene before her. "I want to go to the top of something."

"Well, I'm already near enough to the top of something to suit me," remarked Mrs. Merrill, as she went inside to get warm. "If there's any higher top it will have to get along without me. I'm high enough now."

That idea sounded very agreeable to Mary Jane, for she was beginning to feel very strange. Her face felt stiff as though it was frozen. But she knew she wasn't *that* cold—nowhere near that cold. She decided to say nothing about it—probably it was just a feeling and would go away. But anyway, she didn't want to go to the top of anything more.   She was sure of that.

A guide came into the living room just as the Merrills returned to it and announced that parties would be taken to the Jungfraujoch plateau.

"I'd love to go, Dad," cried Alice. "You know how I love to climb."

"But your clothes, Alice," objected her mother. "You'll freeze, child! And your shoes! Those are good shoes for walking but they were never planned to climb through snow."

"Oh, do let us go, Mrs. Merrill," begged Ellen. "We may never have another chance and we can dry our shoes when we get down. As for being cold, we won't be gone long and we can warm up here by the fire when we get back."

When he saw that Mrs. Merrill still hesitated, Mr. Merrill suggested that they look out over the path to the top and see what conditions were. They went into another room where they saw shoes and mackintoshes and such that could be rented. While they were looking, a party of English people came laughing through the doorway, bringing with them a flurry of snow and cold.

"That was surely jolly!" remarked one English woman, as she changed her coat. "Well worth while!"

Thus encouraged the girls looked out the door and saw a narrow, snow-covered path along the edge of a steep precipice.

"See how simple, mother?" cried Alice, delightedly. "You just steady yourself by this wall—if you need steadying—and follow the guide."

"It certainly doesn't look attractive to me, but then, I don't like precipices, you know. If your father thinks it safe, you may go with him. But Mary Jane and I will stay here and buy pictures while you are gone."

Mary Jane was pleased with that decision but somehow she didn't say anything because her face kept getting stiffer and stiffer. Surely it must show! She put her hand up to it—it felt just as usual to touch. But it didn't feel as usual to smile with. It felt as though it had forgotten how to smile; as though it wouldn't move even if she wanted it to.

Alice and Ellen, with the help of a Swiss saleswoman, were amusing themselves by selecting coats to wear on their climb and shoes that had spikes and would fit. So Mary Jane went back into the main living room where she looked at picture postals and tried to pick out ones she wanted. There was one of the station with the glass window —she would take two of that. And one of the room where she now was standing—of course she wanted that. And one of the view from the balcony and one of the path Alice and Ellen were going to climb. She laid them in a small pile and got out her purse to pay for them.

"Why—Mary Jane Merrill!" cried

Alice's voice. "Whatever is the matter with your face?"

"My face?" asked Mary Jane, weakly. "I thought you were going climbing."

"I am as soon as the guide comes back from taking those other people," said Alice. "But Mother," with careless disregard of what other people might think she called to Mrs. Merrill who was examining some native needlework across the room, "just look at Mary Jane!"

Mrs. Merrill looked. And to her amazement she saw that Mary Jane was a strange color of pea green and her face was twisted as though the muscles were drawn tightly in a way they shouldn't be.

The clerk at the postal card counter looked too—as well as everyone of the few people in the room—and she said, kindly, "The little lady is all right only she feels the altitude. Perhaps she should go down right away. Some people cannot stay up so high and be comfortable. We are nearly twelve thousand feet above the sea here and some find that is pretty high."

Mrs. Merrill had hurried over to Mary Jane as the clerk was talking and put her arm tenderly round her. "Do you feel ill, dear?" she asked.

"No, I'm fine," answered Mary Jane, "only my face is stiff. It doesn't feel as it should."

"Then I think you shouldn't stay another minute," decided Mrs. Merrill, quickly. "When can we get a train down?"

"One is just leaving—if it hasn't already gone," said the clerk, running to the door and calling to the guard. "Wait! More passengers!"

"All aboard quickly, then!" he said, and before Mary Jane hardly knew what was happening to her, some kind person picked up her postal cards (her father paid for them later), some one else held open the door, and Alice helped her on the train while Mr. and Mrs. Merrill made hasty plans—he to take the older girls on their climb and return to Interlaken by a later train, Mrs. Merrill and Mary Jane to go straight to the hotel. And in less than a minute they were off, down the slow climb back to Scheidegg.

It certainly was a good thing that someone noticed Mary Jane just when she did, for the little girl was too proud to complain. Yet if she had had to wait a whole hour for the later train, it wouldn't have been much fun. She and her mother sat still on the return journey and didn't try to see out of windows. As a matter of fact, the snow was now falling so fast that there wasn't much that could be seen anyway.

In a little over an hour they were back at Scheidegg station and Mary Jane's face was all right again. There had been nothing the matter at all except that the Jungfrau was a little too high for her. As the clerk had said up there, some people don't do well up high, others don't feel it a bit.

Mary Jane wanted to stop at Scheidegg and wait till the rest came but the snowstorm was coming on down the mountain. The sky was dark and threatening with rain and Mrs. Merrill thought that their own hotel was the best place for them. So they changed to the Interlaken train which was waiting and went right along. By the time they reached Interlaken the rain was pouring down and they scrambled for a cab and were driven as speedily as possible to the hotel.

There they found a note from Doris asking Mary Jane and Alice for tea. And hardly was the note read before Doris appeared in the office ready to take Mary Jane away. Living in the very next hotel, she had come alone and was thrilled with the thought of going out by herself.

"But my dear!" exclaimed Mrs. Merrill, regretfully, "just look at Mary Jane! Wet and weary and just home from the top of the mountain!"

"She'll feel rested when she has tea," Doris reminded her.

"True enough," admitted Mary Jane's mother with a smile, "tea is a fine idea. Would you be much disappointed if I ordered it up in Mary Jane's room? She could put on her bath-robe and slippers and let her things dry while you ate. And you could have the party all by yourselves just the same."

"Could we, mother?" asked Mary Jane. "They have awfully good things to eat, here," she said to Doris.

"All right, then, let's," said Doris. And the girls started up-stairs.

INTERLAKEN IN THE EVENING

MRS. MERRILL was very particular with her order of "tea"—which really was hot chocolate instead of tea as it would have been in England—for she wanted it to seem like a real party. And in the meantime, Mary Jane took off her damp clothing and while Doris hung it on hangers, she took a quick tub and by the time "tea" arrived, she was warm and cosy in her bathrobe and wrapped up in a woolly blanket for safety. Naturally she had forgotten all about wetness and was telling Doris of her exciting adventure at Lauterbrunnen.

"Tea" was delicious and with it came such an array of little cakes that the girls could hardly decide which to eat first. One was star-shaped with pink icing; one had bits of chocolate sprinkled over the top and baked in. Mary Jane ate those first while Doris chose a square cake with white icing and then a crescent trimmed with green. There was hot toast, too, with honey, which should have been eaten first, and a small pitcher of hot milk and a pot of chocolate so both girls could have "seconds."

Just as they were deciding which cake to eat for the last and which the next to the last, the door-knob rattled and Alice and her father burst in, damp and weary but thrilled with the good time they had had.

"Goodie! Tea!" cried Alice, "I'm famished!"

"But it's gone!" cried Mary Jane, "every single cake but this one and I've had a bite out of it."

"Never mind," said Mrs. Merrill, coming in from her room. "We'll order more at once. Where's Ellen, Alice? Shall we order for her too?"

"No, she stopped at her hotel, mother. And oh, we had the *best* time! We put on heavy shoes—and carried staffs—and walked in the snow—and——"

"Could you see very far?" asked Mary Jane, as she jumped down from the bed and started pulling off Alice's shoes.

"No," replied Alice doubtfully, "not more than four or five mountains, I guess. That's nothing to what you can see sometimes, they told us. But it was fun just the same and I wouldn't have missed it for anything!"

"You must go next time," she added, but Mary Jane was too busy hanging up clothes and putting shoes out to dry to make any promises.

In a very few minutes Alice had had her tub and with the help of Doris and Mary Jane her clothes were all put in order so she could wrap up snugly and enjoy her tea.

To Mary Jane's amazement there were still different sorts of cakes on this tray. Some without any frosting, some with cheese, and some with candied fruit. And of course those all had to be sampled so it was a very satisfying tea she had.

"Now then," said Mrs. Merrill, looking in when she was sure they had finished, "I suppose it's dinner time."

"But mother!" exclaimed Mary Jane, "we've just had tea!"

"Look at your watch, dear. You may just have finished tea, but my watch says ten of six none the less."

"Then I must go," said Doris, "because I was to be at our room before six. We're going on a trip early tomorrow."

"But we'll have another party, sometime, somewhere," said Mary Jane, hopefully. And the girls had had such good luck in running across each other at various places that they said good-by very cheerfully and really expected to meet again soon, even though they didn't know how or where.

"Now, I have a plan," suggested Mrs. Merrill, when Doris had gone, "if you'll look out the window, you'll see that it's much lighter than an hour ago. I think the storm is passing over just as yesterday's did. And I think we can go out this evening and finish our shopping."

"We'd better if we want to leave in the morning," agreed Alice.

"You mean if we *have* to leave," corrected Mary Jane, "we never want to."

"Yes, that's exactly what she means," said Mrs. Merrill. "Now you won't mind having a late dinner after all that tea. I suggest that you two go to your own room and take a rest. Your father and I will write some letters and then we'll have dinner at seven and go shopping afterward. How's that for a plan?"

"Fine," said Mary Jane, "only I'm not sleepy."

"Well, I'm sure you are not hungry, either," said her mother, laughing, "and if you don't rest, we'll have dinner immediately——"

"I guess maybe we had better take naps,

then, Mother," agreed Mary Jane, "because
I really wouldn't know what to order for
dinner right this minute!"

"I'll call you at quarter to seven," promised Mrs. Merrill, as the girls left for their
room. "That will give you time to dress."

Mary Jane had honestly thought she
wasn't sleepy, but, dear me! she didn't
waste any time going to sleep as soon as she
touched the pillow. She slept so soundly
that she almost thought it was morning
when she was called an hour later. It
wasn't easy to get up. You know how it is
after a good nap—it's almost more fun to
keep on napping. She was just about to
say, "Oh, why do we bother to shop?" when
she happened to think of Betty Holden's
little cousin. Of all things to think of suddenly in Interlaken, Switzerland!

"Alice!" she called, sitting up straight
and wide awake in an instant. "We
haven't got any present for Betty's little
cousin who lives in Milwaukee!"

"Well, what of that?" complained Alice sleepily. "We haven't any presents for lots of people yet."

"But I haven't Betty's little cousin on my list and I had forgotten all about her," cried Mary Jane, in distress. "Just think! I might not have remembered even now!"

"Why think about that when you *have* remembered?" responded Alice, practically. "What did you think you'd like to buy for her?" she added, waking up enough now to be interested.

"I thought I'd buy her a dress. You remember Betty's mother said she'd like something we could pick out and she'd buy it when we got home." Mary Jane could see by Alice's expression that she was going to say a dress was too much to buy for a person they hardly knew, so she hurried on to explain.

"Yes, I do remember now," said Alice. "But I'd forgotten all about it too. Suppose we could get one of those pretty smocked dresses? We saw some of them last night. Let's ask mother. I'll beat you dressed, so you'd better hurry."

There was no time for talking then, for even though the girls raced to dress with the race ending in a tie, as it so often did, they had taken so long to wake up that Mr. and Mrs. Merrill were ready and half way down the hall before the girls came to their door. But when dinner was ordered and they were eating the soup, Mary Jane told about her sudden recollection of Betty's request.

"Um-m-m," said Mrs. Merrill thoughtfully. "I don't know about buying things for other people."

"But Betty wanted it so badly," urged Mary Jane.

"Frances spoke of it, too," said Alice, "though I had forgotten all about it. She said to get something nice and that they'd all help Betty pay for it if she couldn't afford it."

"And she'd like a dress," added Mary Jane.

"How old is this little cousin?" asked Mrs. Merrill.

"Two, going on three," replied Mary Jane, "and she takes a three-year size, Betty said so."

"Then we'll see what we can do," agreed Mrs. Merrill. "And if we can't find anything suitable this evening, be sure you put it on your list, Mary Jane, so you don't forget it again. We'll see if we can get something in Florence or in Paris when we go back."

By the time they finished dinner the rain clouds were about out of sight and the evening promised to be very pleasant. Crowds of gay tourists were out strolling and everyone seemed to be in a holiday mood. The Merrills walked across the green to the shops on the other side of the town and then began window-shopping where they left off the evening before. It was such fun.

There were no automobiles—just people—
and a person could dash from one side of the
street to another when this or that window
looked interesting, with never a thought of
traffic.

And the windows! They were as full of
pretty things as the Paris shops. But there
were such different sorts of things that
you'd know in a minute you weren't in
Paris. Laces, ivories, jewelry, carvings,
clocks—oh, such fascinating clocks that did
things as you stood and watched. One
clock was the figure of a small boy and the
face of the clock was on a box which he had
tucked under his arm. When it was time
for the hour to strike he turned his head
gaily from side to side and whistled a tune.
Mary Jane couldn't bear to leave him. The
music box clocks and the cuckoos were interesting enough, but that little fellow
looking for all the world like the boy who
had tried to save her from the goat that
morning, was just too fascinating to leave.

And the obliging shop-keeper turned the clock several times so it could come to the hour and allow the boy to whistle for Mary Jane. Finally her father decided that they were taking far too much of the shop-keeper's time, so he bought some ivory chessmen to take to Mary Jane's grandfather, and they left. Unfortunately the clock was too expensive for their modest pocketbook.

"Here's a shop where they sell dresses," said Alice, who had wandered on while her father's package was being wrapped up. "They look lovely, too."

Of course Mary Jane had to see everything in the windows before they went inside, but as there were several little dresses, smocked gaily in colors, she decided that this was the place to make her purchase. But what do you suppose? The little frocks were not marked with sizes as they would have been in a shop in the United States. The customers had to hold them up and make their own guesses as to whether the size would be right.

"But I don't know how big three years old is?" Mary Jane objected after she had picked out a pretty little dress smocked in blue and just to her liking.

"I'm sure I don't either," said her mother, laughing. "You girls grow up so fast that I forget how big you were at three years. Maybe they can tell us, though.

"Have you any guess about this size?" she asked the mistress of the shop who had been waiting on some other customers till just then.

"Oh, three or four, maybe," she replied, looking at the dress carefully. "What size did you want?"

"For a three-year-old," replied Mary Jane, eagerly.

"Oui, yes," said the woman, "but wait—" And she darted to the back of the shop. The Merrills waited hopefully. In a minute the woman came back, holding by

the hand a pretty little girl with black hair
and beautiful dark eyes.

"She is three; we'll try it on her," explained the woman.

The dress fitted perfectly and the little
girl proudly smoothed it down and turned
round and round to show it off.

"There it is, Madam," said the saleswoman.   "Just right and she is three."

"*Trois, trois, j'ai trois ans*," said the child
in pretty French, as she patted the dress
very proudly and smiled at Mary Jane and
Alice.

"She thinks it is for her," said Alice, regretfully.   "We oughtn't to disappoint her,
mother."

"That's all right," replied the shop-
woman, thinking of her business.   "I shall
tell her."

She squatted down and talked to the
little girl who first seemed sorry, then very
proud and happy.   "I tell her three is such
a big girl that she help me with my business

when people come from the States," she explained.

And as the child seemed pleased and happy, Mary Jane was too. She bought the dress and then grinned at her little Swiss friend while it was being wrapped.

"Good-by," she said, as she tucked the bundle under her arm and went out the door.

" 'By," replied the child and waved gaily. *"Encore!"* she added, and the girls knew that meant, "come again!"

"Mary Jane! Would you look at *that!*"

OVER THE PASS TO LUCERNE

THE Merrills wandered on down the street, window-shopping and enjoying all the sights.

"Mary Jane! Would you look at *that!*" cried Alice, as she rushed over to her sister who was looking in a toy-shop window.

"That" was a dog team pulling a small wagon loaded high with parcels, and guided by a small boy.

"He's delivering things, I know," cried Alice, excitedly. "Let's find what shop he comes from and buy something there that's too big to carry."

"Now if you will tell me, please," said her father, seriously, "how you will carry through Italy and on back to France a package that is too big to carry two blocks to the hotel, I'll buy it for you."

Alice laughed good-naturedly. Of course her father was right. But imagine the fun of telling the girls at home that your store parcels were delivered by a dog team! But at least she could tell them she had watched it being done. So they followed along for a block or two and saw how obedient and well trained the dogs were. They stopped at a word; stood still until told to go and altogether were as perfect as anything could be. The girls were fascinated and only the thought of all the shopping left to do, finally made them turn away.

But the evening would soon be gone. People were already coming from the concert—and Mrs. Merrill had thought that they couldn't go to it because they couldn't be so late! Very quickly they scanned their lists and made a few purchases.

Alice found a carved wooden boy, just the size of Mary Jane's boy with a basket, only this boy was leading a dog instead of carrying grass. Mary Jane found a lovely little pin of ivory carved like a cluster of forget-me-nots and tinted exactly like the ones they had seen on the mountain that morning. Alice bought an ivory pin of edelweiss and Mr. Merrill found a set of checkers matching the chess he had bought earlier. Then of course they got handker-chiefs and lace and postal cards—lots of them—for mailing and for keeping. Just as they were about to leave, Mary Jane found a tiny little ivory dog, just what she liked and fortunately at a price she could afford to pay. So she was very happy.

"There! That's enough shopping for one evening," said Mrs. Merrill. "If we don't get these children home and to bed soon, there won't be any morning! They'll sleep right through it!"

"But mother," said Alice seriously, "we had a nap."

"Yes, and used that up long ago," laughed her mother. "Now let's see who can walk home the quickest."

It was only a little way across to their hotel, fortunately, for as soon as she left the excitement of the stores and bright lights, Mary Jane suddenly felt very sleepy. A little while later, when she was tucked into her soft bed, it felt very, very good to her. This had certainly been an unusually busy day.

At nine the next morning, Mrs. Merrill slipped into the girls' room to call them. Although she spoke several times, they were sleeping so soundly that she decided to let them sleep another hour. It was too bad to waste the time, especially as the sun was shining and the air fresh and fine. But nothing seems fun if a person is too tired— as she was sure the girls had been the day before. So she wrote letters and took a short walk with Mr. Merrill and then called them in earnest this time, at ten.

Once awakened, Alice and Mary Jane were rested and ready to jump right up and enjoy the good breakfast that had been ordered for them.

"Now then," said Mrs. Merrill, "let's pack our bags and let the porter get them whenever he wants to. We won't have to think of a thing but getting ourselves to the train. With all that breakfast, you ought not be hungry till tea and we'll have that in Lucerne late this afternoon. So we can take the rest of the time till our train leaves at twelve-forty to walk and see sights."

Alice and Mary Jane hurried around and picked up their belongings. That didn't take long, for experience was teaching them that it is easier to keep things straight than to waste a lot of time picking up a muss. So their small bags were soon packed and Mary Jane had time to address three picture post cards before her father and mother announced they too were packed and ready to go.

If Mary Jane had thought the shops were the only sights in Interlaken, she surely learned better now. There was a lot to see —lovely gardens, walks with views of the mountains that changed every minute, a band concert on the Strand, and the new baths where crowds of people were enjoying themselves. The baths were the best to watch, Mary Jane thought. There were slides and diving boards and pools for children—all filled with people laughing and shouting and having such a jolly time that it was fun to stand and watch even if you couldn't take part yourself.

"I'd like to stay in Interlaken a whole summer," said Mary Jane, as her mother called the third time for her to start on now. "I liked it when I thought it was just shops; and I like it a lot more now that I've seen the rest of it."

"So do I," agreed her mother, "and I think we'll have to put Interlaken on our list of places to come to again."

"And to stay longer when we do come," added Alice.

"But now we've got to catch that train," said their father, looking at his watch. "And if we don't want to run all the way down the village street, I hope we can get a bus or car or something. Let's hurry over to the street and see what we can find."

They crossed the green to the carriage road and were lucky enough to hail a cab which took them to the station in comfortable time. There they found their luggage which the hotel porter had brought just as promised and they boarded their train with several minutes to spare.

After having been on the highest railroad in the world, Mary Jane no longer felt any fear about traveling over mountain passes. She selected a seat close by the window where she wouldn't miss a single sight, and prepared to enjoy the four or five hour journey to Lucerne.

They rode down the valley past the falls,

along the lake and river, then climbed up the high mountain and through a pass. Maybe in reading about it, the passes and the mountains sound all alike. But in seeing them they seemed very different. Some had very nice, story-bookish houses; some had very shabby homes; some had lots of flowers on green meadows—some rocks, great piles of rocks so hard and bare you'd think there wouldn't be a flower within miles and miles. Sometimes a person could see little children working in the dooryard, feeding chickens, tending the goats, or weeding the garden. Later in the afternoon lots of children were playing. Maybe their work for the day was done and they could play till supper time. It certainly looked that way.

High up on the pass before they went down into the valley where Lucerne is, something happened to the engine. Evidently it wasn't very serious, for the train men didn't appear to be worried or bothered in the least. But it took time to fix. And Mary Jane hadn't had a bite to eat since breakfast. To be sure, breakfast was after ten. But ten o'clock seems a long time away when it is four. Anyone can tell you that—especially if he's hungry. And Mary Jane was. Not only was she hungry—she was hollow clear down to her toes.

Soon the train began to move, but it went slowly, as though experimenting with moving. And just as they reached a pretty little village half way down the mountain it stopped again, though there was no station in sight.

Boys and girls ran back from the station ahead and men and women bobbed up from somewhere—all selling things at the car windows. They had flowers—dainty little bunches of them, fragrant and tempting, and chocolates and fruit. Mary Jane wanted to buy them all. But she looked carefully, for, knowing that she really couldn't buy them *all*, she wanted to be sure she bought what she liked best.

"Can we really buy anything we want, Dadah?" she asked, eagerly.

"You may each buy two things—any two you like," agreed her father.

"Then I want to buy chocolates from that boy over there," said Mary Jane, pointing to a smiling boy about Alice's age who had a very pretty basket full of neatly wrapped chocolates. "And I want some fruit—" She looked along the train at the many vendors while her father bought the chocolates. Down by the next car she spied an old woman who carried a tray on her arm. On this were piles of tiny baskets, each filled with fruit.

Just then the old woman happened to look Mary Jane's way and, seeing her interest, she hurried to the window.

"Fruit? Fruit? Fruit?" she asked.

Mary Jane didn't know the word and couldn't even tell whether it was French or German—it seemed like either and probably was dialect.   But the woman held up the dainty baskets of freshly washed fruit as she spoke, and any little girl could tell what she was saying by those.

The baskets were made of twisted twigs and lined with fresh green leaves.   And each basket contained apricots, ripe cherries, and strawberries arranged with a nice feeling for color combination that made a very pretty effect.

"Oh, Dadah," cried Mary Jane, "this is what I want most.   Aren't they lovely?"

"They surely are and we'll take four," said Mrs. Merrill.   Much to her delight, Mary Jane had the fun of picking out four baskets.   She choose two with apricots on top, one with cherries, and one with a great strawberry—probably about the last of the season.   Of course the fruit down in the basket was about the same in each, but the varieties on top made the baskets look different.

Mr. Merrill paid the money through the open window just as the train started to move away. It crawled along very slowly the rest of the way to Lucerne and arrived there an hour late. But Mary Jane didn't care a bit. She ate all her share of the chocolate and her whole basket of fruit. She packed the basket very carefully in her hat box because she wanted to take it home to show to Betty Holden. And with that, the delayed tea wasn't such a serious matter as it otherwise would have been. You know yourself how that is.

SUNDAY IN LUCERNE

WHEN their train did finally pull into the station at Lucerne, Mary Jane was amazed to see how big a city it was. Montreux and Interlaken had been such cosy, small towns that, without realizing it, she had come to think that all Swiss towns were like that. But this station was big—as large as the stations in cities at home. There were many trains and lots of people and a jabber of French, German, and Italian that was very confusing to a little girl.

She was glad to see the uniform and cap of the travel bureau's man and to know that someone was meeting them and looking after the Merrills in this strange city.

Standing close by her mother, she waited till the luggage was put on the top of a bus marked with the name of their hotel. Then she climbed in and found a seat way up in front near the driver. Many other people got in, too, so that the bus was quite full when it set off at a jolly pace, out of the station and down the broad street.

They rode past buildings and parks and street cars and motors, past bridges and monuments and more parks and along a lake—oh, it was quite a journey from the station to their hotel. But finally they pulled up before a very nice looking building and people began to get out.

"Let's see our rooms before we look around," Mary Jane suggested as they went through the lobby. "Maybe we could look around better after dinner. Perhaps it's almost dinner time now," she added hopefully.

"Yes, lets," agreed Alice. "I'm sure this is going to be a good hotel. I think all Switzerland hotels are nice."

Their rooms which had been engaged in

advance were all ready for them, so Mary
Jane could have her wish and go right up.
They had two connecting rooms on the
front overlooking the lake and the mountains and glaciers beyond. The girls
thought the view was the loveliest they had
yet had from their windows and Alice immediately began planning the pictures she
would take.

Mary Jane wasn't interested in pictures.
She saw something she hadn't seen for *days*
—something that interested her more at
that minute than—well, than all the views
in the world. And what do you suppose
that something was? A washstand with
running water—right there in her own
room! Of course it was fun to ring for
water, to have a pretty, daintily dressed
maid bring up a pitcher of hot water when
you wanted it. That was part of the fun
of traveling in strange countries. But to
have water when you wanted it just by
turning on a faucet—why that was like

home! Mary Jane was so thrilled she didn't even want to see the glacier Alice was pointing out.

She hurried to the washstand and turned on the faucet—yes, the water came. Doubtfully she turned on the other and stuck her finger under the water. Cold. Well, sometimes it started out cold at home. She'd let it run a minute. Soon it got warmer—warmer—finally it was hot and she turned off the waste and drew a bowlful. It was such fun to make suds and scrub, knowing that when that water got cold or soiled you could get plenty more!

Mary Jane took off her traveling dress and scrubbed some more until finally Alice got tired of looking at views and demanded her turn. And then they had the biggest surprise of all. Over in the other corner, half hidden by a screen, was *another* wash stand so each person in the room could have one of her own.

"I'd like to stay at this hotel a while,"

said Mary Jane, gaily, when the discovery was made. "Or anyway, if we can't stay, I wish we could take the wash stands with us. Is there something I could wash for you, Alice?" she asked, looking at her spotless hands disappointedly. There really wasn't any reason for washing such clean hands *again*.

"Yes, indeed there is," replied Alice. "You can wash my gloves and three pairs of stockings."

"Goody! You get them out and I'll do them this very minute," said Mary Jane, happily.

But that plan was spoiled by Mr. Merrill coming to their door with the remark, "Dinner is served in two minutes and the placard on my door says guests are expected to be prompt. Are you ready?"

"In a jiff!" cried Mary Jane, "I'll just smooth my hair so—and slip on my dress so —and here I am." There she was, clean and fresh and ready to go down-stairs.

The dining room was a large, cheerful room gaily lighted with many lights that sparkled and shone in their crystal holders. The tables were set with pretty linen and china and glass and it looked very promising. All the guests came in at the same time, and the head waiter, standing at one side, waited until everyone was seated. Then stepping to the wall, he pressed a button and out from a door came a score of waiters, each carrying trays of steaming soup.

"It's like the story of Aladdin," said Mary Jane, gleefully. "Don't you remember how he rubbed the lamp and then things happened—all at once?"

The soup—a thick, creamy kind—was delicious, and Mary Jane ate hers down to the last drop. Then she looked around to see what would happen next.

The head waiter watched the guests and when all had finished their soup, he pressed the button again and the whole lot of waiters came in again, removed the soup plates, and brought the next course. The food was delicious and there were many, many courses because only one or two things were served together. There was a separate course for cauliflower and another separate course for green beans. The dessert was a pudding of sugar and spice and cream, and after that there was a course of crackers and cheese—several kinds of cheese so one could surely find a kind that pleased.

Of course Mary Jane didn't know there would be so *many* courses. How could she? And of course, being hungry as always, she ate heartily of the first few. So by the time the pudding and later the cheese came, she was more interested in watching the waiters and the guests than she was in eating. You wouldn't be surprised at that! The waiters served every course at the tap of the bell and were so quiet and skilful that they seemed like well drilled soldiers.

Among the guests were people from many countries. At the table next to the Merrills there was a party of Germans who talked so vigorously in their language that Mary Jane thought that maybe they were quarreling. But she soon found they weren't; they were having a beautiful time telling each other stories and laughing in between. It was only the fact that they spoke in a strange language that made their talk sound queer to a little girl who didn't know that tongue. She couldn't help wishing that she had learned two or three languages as little English girls do.

After dinner the guests had coffee in the lounge where a roaring fire made the room seem home-like and jolly. Of course it was summer, but here in the mountain country there was a chill after the sun had set, and a fire seemed very pleasant.

"Shall we go for a walk?" asked Mrs. Merrill, presently.

"I think I should wash my hands before we do anything else," said Mary Jane. "Have you the key to our room, Dadah?"

"Don't wash too long," laughed Mrs. Merrill, "or there'll be no time for walking. I suggest that as we are going to be here over tomorrow, certain little girls whom I shall not mention had better turn in early and get some beauty sleep. They've almost forgotten what a real bedtime is."

"Why, it isn't more than half past seven, Mother!" exclaimed Mary Jane.

"Look at your watch and see," replied Mrs. Merrill.

Mary Jane looked. To her amazement, she found that it said quarter to nine! Evidently serving dinner in lots of courses took time. But where it had gone to, she couldn't see! That was because she was having such fun watching everything and there hadn't been a minute to be bored.

"Maybe we'd better not go walking," she said. "I've some washing to do."

"Washing!" exclaimed her mother. "Well, that's all right. But you don't have to announce it from the house-tops, child! Why not wait until tomorrow and take a little walk now?"

Mary Jane couldn't think of a better plan so she and Alice hurried up-stairs and washed their hands, got hats and coats, and hurried down again to discover their parents talking with some English people.

"Come here, dear," said Mrs. Merrill to Mary Jane, "and see who we have come across. Do you remember seeing these people at the Riggs Crown Hotel?"

Mary Jane didn't. Really, she had been so busy at Windermere, playing with the Wilson children (friends they had met on the boat) that she didn't remember noticing anyone else. But she couldn't be rude and say that. So she just smiled and held out her hand and the lady didn't seem to notice any omission.

"They remembered us," continued Mrs. Merrill, "and have been telling us about some of the trips we should choose from for tomorrow. I think I like the boat ride the best. Would you, Mary Jane?"

Mary Jane thought she would and said so. But she wished she knew if there were any children who belonged to the English lady. Especially any little girls about her own age. It would be fun to have such a person along on a boat trip.

Then she remembered her washing plans.

"Would the boat take *all* day, Mother?" she asked, anxiously. "And would we have to go early?"

Her mother smiled knowingly as she replied, "We won't take one that goes too early, and we won't be gone all day. I know you have some other things to do. We'll wait till morning and see the weather and decide then. But we're glad to know about what there is to do, just the same."

Chatting together, they all went out the door and walked down the street, Alice and Mary Jane going together behind the others. But Mary Jane was more weary than she had thought and soon lagged farther and farther behind. So Mr. Merrill walked back with her to the hotel. They hadn't gone half way when Alice ran and caught up with them. She had decided to turn in, too.

The last thing before she snuggled down under the covers Mary Jane said, "Now Alice, before you get into bed, put out your stockings and gloves where I can see them. Dadah says tomorrow is Sunday, but I'm going to pretend it's Monday. I plan to get up early in the morning and get our washing done."

And then, quick as her head touched the pillow, she went to sleep.

THE LEGEND OF WILLIAM TELL

BUT the sun, which Mary Jane had counted on awakening her the next morning, didn't do his duty. In fact, hidden behind a bank of rain clouds, he didn't even look at Lucerne till the late afternoon, and then only for a few minutes. The morning was so dark that when Mary Jane did waken, she thought it was almost the middle of the night and went right back to sleep again. Finally, the ringing of a bell made her look at her watch and she found it was nine o'clock. And here she had planned to be up early!

"Alice!" she called to the sleeping figure in the bed close by, "Alice! We'd better wake up! Perhaps they serve breakfast all at once, same as dinner and maybe it's already too late to get any!" Such a dreadful thought made Mary Jane jump out from the cosy covers and run to the door of her parents' room.

They were up and dressing and her father reassured her by saying that breakfast was served at three different hours and that they would be in plenty of time if they went down soon.

Breakfast wasn't served in the regular dining room but in a small sun-porch overlooking the lake. No doubt on a sunny morning there would be a lovely view from the tables, but this morning all one could see was rain. Rain came down so steadily and heavily that it made what little one could view of the lake look just like a part of the rain.

But Mary Jane didn't mind. Why should she? For there on the table was a bowl from which she could take her pick of fresh fruit. Here also was a jar of honey big enough even for a person who was very, very fond of honey. And as she sat down, the waiter brought a great pitcher of hot chocolate and a plate of crisp, hot rolls. Who would care about rain in a case like that?

But the grown-ups seemed to be bothered. "This is the only time we'll have the lake trip," said Mrs. Merrill, disappointedly.

"And I have a whole list of places I wanted to see in the city," said her father, "including a church where we could attend the service."

"Well, I don't care if I stay right here all day," said Mary Jane comfortably, as she reached for another roll. "I think it's lovely here and I don't care about lakes or cities or anything like that."

"Maybe that would be a good plan," said Mrs. Merrill thoughtfully. "She has been doing a lot and maybe it would be better to have her stay right here at the hotel as she wants to. Would you be lonesome, Mary Jane?"

Before she could reply, the English lady

stopped by their table as she left the room and remarked, "Our little girl is staying here with her governess this morning, while we go sight-seeing. Would your little girl like to stay with her?"

Would she? Mary Jane beamed. Ordinarily, Mary Jane liked seeing sights as much as anyone. But today was different —with rain outside and such a nice hotel inside. So, to make a long story short, the English lady brought her little daughter Natalie and her governess, Miss Throup, to the lounge to meet Mary Jane and her family. Although both girls were a little shy of each other at first, they soon had a smiling acquaintance.

"Mary Jane had some things she wants to do in her room," said Mrs. Merrill, as plans were being made. "Suppose we say that she will be down here in an hour."

"Maybe an hour and a half," said Mary Jane, who didn't want to be hurried with her washing.

"All right," agreed her mother, "an hour and a half. That would be eleven-thirty. Would you and Natalie be here then, Miss Throup?"

"We'll be here all morning," said Miss Throup. "And we shall be delighted to see Mary Jane any time she comes down."

So plans were made and the Merrills went to their rooms to make ready.

Mary Jane searched through her bags and finally succeeded in discovering three pairs of stockings of her own. Those, with Alice's, made a fair sized washing and so she busily set to work. First she strung the line across from the bed to a chair. She hadn't used that line for days and it was fun to get it out again—almost as much fun as the time she and Alice had played and washed in their castle-like room in Edinburgh, Scotland. Next she put the clothespins on the table where she could get them quickly when the things were ready to be hung up.

Now it was time to take off her good dress, to get the little package of soap flakes from her mother's hat box and the fun could begin.

When Mr. and Mrs. Merrill and Alice bade her good-by, she was in the midst of trying to get a good Chicago-like suds out of Lucerne water. She found this such a task that good-bys were very brief. Mary Jane didn't even think of being sorry she had decided not to go along.

Finally all the stockings and two pairs of gloves were beautifully clean and perfectly rinsed and hung on the line—toes up and papers on the floor under them so they wouldn't drip on the carpet. Mary Jane dried her hands and looked at her watch. Eleven o'clock. Then there was half an hour before she was to go down-stairs— none too much time for her hair must be made tidy and a fresh dress put on.

"Just at that minute the maid came in to "do" the room and make the beds. Although she couldn't speak English, she and Mary Jane soon struck up a smiling friendship and the maid had a good laugh over the washing.

Miss Throup and Natalie were looking for Mary Jane when she came down-stairs just on time. They took her over to a cosy window-seat, overlooking the lake, where they had been sitting.

"We like this place," said Miss Throup, "because we think from here we can see the place where William Tell landed when he made his escape."

"Escape?" asked Mary Jane in surprise, "who ran away? Can I see him now?"

"Goodness, no!" laughed Miss Throup. "William Tell lived—let me see—about six hundred years ago. Don't you know about him, dear?"

Mary Jane shook her head. Naturally she hated to admit that she didn't know about something she was evidently supposed to know. But she had long since discovered that if you don't know something, it's better to admit it than to pretend. Sometimes by pretending to know, a person misses hearing a very good story that would be fun to hear.

"No," she said, frankly, "I don't know anything about any William Tell nor his escaping or any such thing."

"Then you must tell her right away," cried Natalie, happily, "and I'll hear it all over again."

"That will suit you, won't it, dear?" laughed Miss Throup, then turning to Mary Jane she added, "such a girl for stories you never saw! She likes them old and she likes them new and she'll be glad to have an excuse for hearing this one over again because it's a favorite.

"Before I begin," continued Miss Throup, "I want you both to look out of the window and pretend you can see only what I tell you. All these hotels and churches and houses will be gone—they have all been put up since the day of William Tell. And the streets and street cars and motors and wagons—all gone—we don't see even a hint of such things."

"But we can see the mountains and the lake," said Mary Jane, entering into the fun of the imagining.

"Exactly," agreed Miss Throup, "we can see all those. And the trees and the glaciers——"

"Only we can't really see those because of the rain," Natalie objected.

"True, only you know they are there, so you can see them in your mind," said Miss Throup. "Just that way you can see the other things I tell you now.

"See a small town of wooden houses— Swiss houses but perhaps more gaily painted than those you saw yesterday around Interlaken, Mary Jane. And see a market square down near the covered bridge. You must see that bridge before you leave, Mary Jane. See it even though it does rain. And at the market place—a big open square—see lots of people in homespun clothes. Some of the men are on horseback, but most of them are a-foot and going about their business.

"This country here had been under Austrian rule and the local ruler at the time of our story was a cruel man named Gesler —he's the villain of our story so don't forget his name. He was a very vain man and in order to get homage from the people he commanded that his hat should be put upon a pole in the market place down the street there and that everyone who passed should kneel in homage before it.

"Of course that irritated the Swiss people for they were used to being very independent. But they had no choice in the matter; they could kneel or go to prison—perhaps even be killed.

"One day William Tell had to go to the village on business and he took his little son with him for the journey. Tell was a fine archer and a good citizen much liked by everyone who knew him. As he and his son were starting, Mrs. Tell called to him, 'Don't forget, William. The pole is in the market place. Go you around some other way.' And he promised that he would.

"But the day was fine and Tell and his son were talking and first thing they knew they were in the village—and there was the pole. Of course William Tell would not kneel down before a hat—that seemed just silly to him. So he walked sturdily by and ordinarily would have been safe enough, for the villagers would not have told tales— they liked Tell too well for that! But alas, Gesler himself happened by at that minute.

" 'Halt!' he shouted, 'who goes by without bowed head and bent knee?'

" 'William Tell, your honor!' Tell said, kneeling willingly enough before a person. It was the farce of a hat he hated.

" 'Kneel before the hat!' shouted Gesler, but not a move did Tell make.

" 'Take him to prison!' ordered the ruler.

"Before they went to get Tell, someone said to Gesler, 'He is a fine soldier and a perfect archer. Shall we take him none-theless?' The people hated to see such a fine man as Tell put in prison on a silly charge.

" 'No,' Gesler said, with a sudden cruel thought, 'let him shoot his way to freedom. Put an apple on yonder child's head and let him shoot it off if he is so good a marksman.'

" 'But sire!' cried the guard in horror, 'the boy is his son!'

" 'What matters, if he is so good a marksman?' the cruel Gesler jeered.

"So Tell had no choice. Trembling, he took his bow and arrow while guards grabbed his little son, set him against a tree a hundred paces away, and put a ripe apple on his head.

" 'Don't be afraid, father!' shouted the boy. 'You can do it! You won't hit me! See? I am not afraid!' "

"Oh, I've heard that story," cried Mary Jane, "I remember now. I just forgot his name."

"Of course you have," said Miss Throup, "I was sure you would remember. So you know how it ended. Tell, trembling though he was, shot the arrow and smashed the apple on his son's head. But even that did not satisfy Gesler. He ordered Tell taken prisoner and with him they put out in a boat to cross the lake. A storm came up— you know how suddenly the mountain storms do come—and only Tell was brave enough to direct the rowers. He gave them a certain course and when they got close to the shore—over there where you can see, girls—he leaped from the boat, shoved it away with his foot and dashed off into the forest to safety. And so well liked was he that no one would tell Gesler where he could be found. So he wasn't recaptured."

"Is it a true story?" asked Natalie.

"It's supposed to be," replied Miss

Throup, "and even though it may not be literally true, it is true of the courage and pluck of the Swiss people."

"And it's true that there are the lake and the stone and the market place, too," added Mary Jane, "so that's true enough for us, it seems to me."

ON TO LUGANO

"NOW tell us another one—please!" said Mary Jane when she had finished asking all the questions she could think of about William Tell. And obliging Miss Throup told more of the many interesting stories, some history and some legend, about the Swiss people. Because they are brave and courageous and also because the rugged condition of their country makes many hardships, there are many, many tales which you can read for yourself in books about Switzerland if you are interested. Mary Jane was. And she resolved that when she got home she would learn more stories, more than could be told in a morning or a day.

"Now then," said Miss Throup, finally, "I think that's enough for one time. What did your mother tell you that you were to do after we had had our visit?"

"I was to eat my luncheon at the table where we had breakfast. The waiter knows about me, because mother told him to look after me—I heard her. And then I am to go up to my room, take off my shoes and dress and wrap up in a woolly blanket she laid out, and take a nap." Mary Jane recited it carefully, and showed how well she had paid attention to what her mother said.

"My child!" exclaimed Miss Throup, "you certainly remember well. And it's a nice plan, too. I shouldn't mind it myself. And we certainly would do the same thing ourselves, Natalie and I, if we had been traveling as you have, my dear."

"But we haven't had luncheon yet and she doesn't have to take her nap till after that," Natalie reminded her governess. "Can't we eat now?"

"We certainly can," said Miss Throup.

"It's just one and I think that by the time you two have washed your hands and made yourselves tidy, the luncheon bell will ring—maybe it will even before you are ready, so skip along with you!"

The girls needed no second bidding, but hurried up the stairs companionably. Luncheon was a delicious meal, informal like breakfast, and the three had a very gay time while eating. Then Mary Jane said good-by promptly and ran up to her room while Natalie and Miss Throup went back to the lounge to watch for Natalie's mother who was to be back very soon.

Mary Jane found her washing still very wet. The rain outside and the lack of heat inside made drying clothing a very slow process.

"It's a good thing we don't have to pack up and leave here this evening," she said to herself as she squeezed out some water from each stocking. "Maybe now that that's out and they have a lot more time, they'll be dry." Whereupon she crept under the dripping line over to her bed and spread over her the blanket that was neatly folded at the foot.

She had thought it would be hard work to go to sleep, but it wasn't. In fact, it would have been very hard work to stay awake. She said over to herself the story of William Tell. But she got only as far as the arrival of Tell and his son to the village square when she dropped off, sound to sleep.

At a quarter to four Alice arrived and waked her up.

"Oh, Mary Jane," said Alice, "we've had such fun. But I'm wet as a sop. I guess it was a good thing you didn't go—though I'd have liked it better if you had! But as soon as I get some dry clothes on, I want to take you back to the wooden bridge that we saw!"

"I saw that, too, when we came from the station yesterday," said Mary Jane.

"Yes, so did I," Alice reminded her. "But I didn't see the inside. I thought it was just any wooden bridge that was very old. But it isn't. It's a very special bridge with colored pictures painted in panels on the inside—like—like—well, I don't know what it's like. Nothing I have ever seen before, I know that!"

"Are they pretty pictures?" asked Mary Jane, rubbing her eyes.

"No-o-o, I wouldn't really call them pretty," said Alice thoughtfully, "they're of angels and devils and saints and——"

"On a *bridge?*" cried Mary Jane, incredulously.

"Yes, on a bridge," said Alice, "the strangest bridge you ever saw. Mother and Dad are going back with us so I can see it better and you can too." While she talked she was changing as quickly as she could, and Mary Jane, interested now even though it was hard work to wake up, dressed too, and soon they were off.

They walked down the street a half mile or so to the park by the edge of the lake. There great high trees had kept off the rain so the ground was dry underneath. Now that the storm had cleared away, crowds of people were going walking. The beautiful old trees, the water at the edge of the park and the crowds of foreign people, all enjoying themselves and their families, made Mary Jane think of Lincoln Park at home in Chicago. She had been there sometimes on a Sunday, so she knew this was very like that place.

"Do you suppose any of these people have ever been in Lincoln Park?" she asked her father.

"I couldn't say, Pussy," he replied, interested in her idea, "but I am sure that if they did come, they'd feel very much at home—all but missing the mountains—because the lake and park and the trees and people would seem like home."

They walked on in the park to the end

where the lake turned into a river and wandered off through the valley. Across this river, angle-wise, was the wooden bridge which was just as fascinating as Alice had said it was. The floor was of great wooden planks, there were sides and posts supporting a roof, and up there in the roof, in the ceiling part of it, were the paintings. The girls looked at many and tried to decipher their strange pictured meanings, but they were so faded and so high overhead that a person would have to peer a long time to see them all.

"And you'd have to lie down on the floor to look up at them," added Mary Jane, after she had stretched her neck a while. "But if you don't look too hard, but just enough to see how jolly they are, they're fun, I think."

So the Merrills walked down the whole length of the bridge and window-shopped in some nice looking little stores and then walked back again. Mary Jane liked looking at the river as well as at the paintings. It flowed along under the low bridge so silently and so swiftly, paying no attention to people or bridges. She dropped a bit of paper she found on the bridge and— would you believe it?—that paper was gone. It disappeared under the bridge and was gone down the river by the time she dashed across to see it from the other side. That showed how fast the current was.

Walking back from the bridge, Mr. Merrill hailed a cab and took the girls for a short drive around the city. They saw beautiful buildings of a very different style from any they had seen thus far—the architecture was German, the driver said. They saw many fine monuments, more parks, and altogether they got a very good idea of the city. Then they went back to the hotel in time for dinner which was served as on the night before.

A second time, Mary Jane felt very used to the waiters coming and going on the signal of the bell, and thought it was a fine plan, for everyone was served at once. But on the other hand, you couldn't see what dessert the people next to you were having while you ate your soup. That made it harder to decide which dessert to order when the time came for deciding. Fortunately a person had to decide only between two and each time Mary Jane chose pudding because she knew what that word was on the menu. And usually she liked it, so that was all right. The times she didn't like pudding, she had fruit and crackers and cheese anyway, and so she never went hungry.

Next morning the stockings were dry enough to be packed, and Mary Jane gathered up all her belongings before breakfast, as she knew they were to take a ten o'clock train. For that reason, she had time to go with Alice to visit a garden near the hotel on the side of the lake, while her mother and father finished their packing. But even though the flowers were lovely, the girls could only stay ten minutes. Then it was bus time, and off they went to the station.

"Now where is it we are going now?" asked Mary Jane, when they had found their reserved seats and arranged their luggage in the rack overhead.

"To Lugano," replied her mother, "and unless we have been told very wrongly, you are going to find it different from Lucerne and Interlaken. But you'll like it very much."

"Lugano," repeated Mary Jane. "It sounds as though I'd like it. When do we get there, mother?"

"Not until two o'clock. We have luncheon on this train. Watch for the tunnels. There'll be many, and one of them is the longest tunnel in Europe."

ICES AND PEACOCKS

THE journey to Lugano was one of the pleasantest the Merrills had had. Mary Jane enjoyed it all the more because she was used to traveling over the mountains now and didn't feel afraid of the heights. It seemed to her that after the trip to the Jungfraujoch nothing would ever seem high again. The mountain passes that would have frightened her terribly the day she left Montreux, now seemed fun to see. And the tunnels that at first appeared gloomy and scary, now only interested her because she and Alice were counting them, seeing how many they could get on a trip.

Most of the tunnels were short, lasting— well, maybe for as long as a person could count twenty or thirty. They came so suddenly. She would be looking at the mountains or valleys or houses or clouds and, presto, they would be gone. There wouldn't be any mountains or clouds or anything—only blackness, out of the window. About half way along their journey they flashed into a tunnel and Mary Jane cried "Fifteen!" and sat back to wait a minute till they came out again.

But they didn't come out. They traveled on and on and on, through the pitchy blackness. It seemed hours, though of course it was only minutes.

"I think this must be the tunnel under the St. Gothard Pass," said Mr. Merrill's voice from the darkness. "It's the longest tunnel we'll be in and this certainly seems to be that."

"Are we stuck or anything?" asked Alice anxiously. "We seem to be going all right."

"We are," her father assured her. "We're traveling along at a lively clip.

But it's a long tunnel—five miles or more if I recall rightly. And just think, this pass that we go under in these few dark minutes, is the same pass that many an army has struggled to climb. Men have died by hundreds in the dangers of this pass—called the gateway from north to the south of Switzerland."

Mary Jane didn't fancy thinking about such serious facts while they were traveling through the darkness. Dark seems so much darker, when thoughts are gloomy.

"Do you suppose we can have luncheon in this dark?" she asked, dolefully.

"No, I don't think that would be very nice," replied her father, "but as soon as we get through here, we'll go into the restaurant car. The travel bureau advised that it would be better not to be in the car during the tunnel."

"Heavens! I should say so!" exclaimed Alice. "Just imagine having food in front of you now and wondering how many cinders were getting into the potatoes! I'd much rather be here."

Mary Jane wasn't so sure she agreed, but she sat still, looking out at the window. Of course, she couldn't see a thing when she did look; only now and then there came a red light, or the flash of a flare along the track.

Then suddenly, just as she was about giving up expecting it, they were in the sunshine and she was blinking surprisingly at the brilliance of it. Trees were gay with green, the flowers were brighter than any they had seen and, as soon as the chill of the tunnel left their compartment, the air was warmer than any they had felt in Switzerland.

"Isn't it lovely and *summer!*" exclaimed Mary Jane, "and *now* do we have luncheon?"

"Right this minute," said her mother, and they started for the restaurant car at once.

The meal was excellent, but the thing that pleased Mary Jane most was the basket of delicious fruit which the waiter set before them as their last course. It contained oranges and limes and strawberries and apricots and green almonds, the first Mary Jane had tried to eat. Of course she remembered the almonds that a person bought at the grocery at Thanksgiving time. These were the same sort of almonds, only picked green so that the flavor was entirely different— tart and snappy and very good, the girls thought.

Mary Jane ate two and then her mother suggested that perhaps two was plenty for the first time, so she ate an orange and an apricot. She couldn't decide which was the better, because both were so very good.

Promptly at two o'clock they arrived at Lugano and Mary Jane liked it from the first minute she saw it from the train. She liked the way two great mountains stood like guards on each side of the bay; she liked the town settled so cosily on the side of the lake; she liked the gay roofs of the houses and the many trees, and, most of all, she liked their hotel, which was up the hill from the railroad, overlooking everything.

"And look at our rooms!" Mary Jane exclaimed, happily, as they were shown into two charming rooms in the front, overlooking the bay and mountains. "And our balcony and everything!" she added, as she discovered a narrow balcony connecting their rooms.

She stepped out from her room and ran along the balcony to the window of her mother's room. From there, she came back through the door connecting the two rooms and went back to the balcony again. A person could run a regular merry-go-round in that way or play hide and seek or any such game as easily as not.

"But let's not stop here," said Alice, who reluctantly came in from the balcony when her mother suggested that they open bags and refresh themselves. "Let's go walking first and unpack after a while."

"That's not such a poor suggestion, at that," her father said, approvingly. "I rather think that if you saw your face you might decide to wash, Alice," he added, laughing. "But as for unpacking, let's forget it until we've explored the town. It's two-fifteen now—or fourteen-fifteen as our friends here would say. Let's see who can be down at the front door, ready to go at fourteen and a half."

"I'll be there," said Mary Jane, pulling her dress off over her head as she spoke. She rang for hot water, for there was no running water here. Lucerne had been a very special exception.

"Me, too," said Alice, looking into her bag for soap, "you just watch me hurry!" And sure enough, in fifteen minutes they were off, walking down the hillside toward the town.

"I wonder if we can shop any today," said

Alice, who counted yesterday lost because she hadn't bought a thing.

"Oh, I've left my purse on my dresser!" exclaimed Mary Jane, suddenly remembering.

"Better run right back and get it, Pussy," said her mother quickly. "It isn't right to leave money around in a hotel. And you might need it while we are out."

So Mary Jane ran back up the hill into the hotel and up the stairs as fast as she could hurry. Just as she was opening her door, the maid who had brought the hot water came out.

"Oh," said Mary Jane breathlessly, "I've left my purse! Is it there yet?"

"Of course, Miss," said the maid, quickly. "It's right on the dresser over there where you left it. And it would be quite safe, Miss. You need have no concern. This is Switzerland, a land of honest people." She said it so proudly that Mary Jane was a bit ashamed of her hurry till she remembered that she was getting her purse, not really because it might be stolen but more because she might want to use it shopping.

"It's a very nice land, I like it," she agreed with the maid. "We're having a lovely time here and maybe we'll want to buy some souvenirs, so I need my money."

The maid grinned happily and replied, "Yes, Miss!" so Mary Jane took the purse and hurried back down the hill to overtake her family.

Down they walked and down, through winding stairs and down streets that were stairsteps—can you imagine anything stranger? Till they came to the edge of the lake where there was a wide driveway around the bay.

"Shall we get a carriage?" Mr. Merrill asked the girls.

"Oh, let's walk a while more," said Alice. "We haven't walked much lately and I can see so much more if we go slowly."

So they walked on and on—under trees that were almost as tropical as some they remembered in Florida, past gardens and houses and inviting spots till at last they came to a park where they sat down to rest. All around were blooming bushes, flower beds, and trees, and some of them were filled with blooms. In front of them the lake, dotted here and there with boats, looked blue and sparkling in the hot sunshine.

From behind there came a strange sound. Mary Jane whirled around to see and there were two beautiful peacocks, spreading their tails and preening themselves in the sunshine. Alice said not a word but turned her camera and snapped a picture while Mary Jane looked and admired. The Merrills sat very still and the peacocks came up quite close. They didn't seem as shy as those at Warwick Castle, but behaved as though they were used to being petted and paid attention to by strangers. But the minute Mary Jane thought of stroking one and stood up to go to him, the pair of them snapped their tails together and hurried off with loud sounds of disgust.

"There now," exclaimed Mary Jane, disappointedly, "Why did I do that?"

"Never mind, dear," said Alice, "we've sat here a long time anyway. Let's walk back to the main street and see if we can find a shop or two. We haven't shopped at a single window yet today."

"If you could wait till after tea," suggested Mrs. Merrill, "I'd suggest that we go back to that nice-looking place where we saw tables under those gay awnings on the sidewalk. But maybe you're in too big a hurry——"

"She isn't in a hurry at all," said Mary Jane, "are you Alice? 'Cause there's plenty of time for her to shop after tea."

But "tea" turned out to be ices; Mary Jane had three before she stopped. That isn't as greedy as it sounds for an ice was

served in a little silver dish and the portion
was small and dainty. Mary Jane had first
a strawberry, then a lemon and then another
strawberry because she decided she liked it
the better. With the ices, Mrs. Merrill ordered cakes and the maid brought a generous plateful of pretty little frosted cakes
that looked more like candies than cakes.

"We might as well eat them all up now
that we've got them," said Alice, as she
helped herself after having had several.
"You'll have to pay for them all anyway."

But, as they soon found out, that wasn't
the way it was done in Lugano. When they
had finished, the waiter came out and carefully counted the cakes that were left (only
two!), and charged them for those they had
eaten.

"That's a funny way to make out a
check!" laughed Mary Jane, "to count
what's left! Wouldn't he have been surprised if nothing were there?"

"Maybe not," said her father, "maybe he's seen hungry little girls before."

Mr. Merrill paid the bill and called a cab, for they had had quite a bit of walking. He told the driver to take them around the bay and then back to some good stores for the ladies.

A FAREWELL PARTY

"THIS is just the kind of street I want to walk on!" exclaimed Alice when they strolled along after their drive. "That's like the pictures, Dadah. Do let's turn here!"

Mary Jane looked up the street where her sister pointed. It was narrow—narrower than the alley back of their apartment at home. Three and four story buildings rose high on each side, shutting out the hot sun and making a fresh coolness that seemed very pleasant. Over the sidewalks were stone porches—no, that wasn't it at all, she found on looking closer. The sidewalks were under a part of the buildings, for the upper stories went out over the porches that covered the walks.

On the walks, under these columned

Mary Jane looked up the street where her sister pointed.

roofs sat women, fat and old, .guarding
baskets of vegetables and fruits which they
begged people to buy. Passing along the
street, almost bumping the girls sometimes
(for the way was so narrow), other women
came and went, carrying on their backs
great heavy baskets full of garden stuff,
fresh and green and tempting. But of
course the Merrills couldn't buy beans or
greens or apricots or limes when they were
not housekeeping. So they strolled on.

Soon they came to a district of shops
where shawls and jewelry and leather goods
and linens were displayed. But, to Alice's
disappointment, there wasn't much in the
windows—not as in Paris or Interlaken.
Instead, the doors were wide open archways
and one wandered in and out of shops looking around as one pleased. The girls hesitated to do this even though the shopkeepers
invited them with smiles and bows and cor-
dial gestures.

"Here's a shawl like the one you've been

looking for!" exclaimed Alice, eagerly, as she peeped into one shop and saw some shawls spread along the counter. "See, Mother? It's just the color you wanted!"

While Mrs. Merrill went inside to see, Mary Jane wandered on to the next shop where there weren't any shawls or dresses. Here instead there were postal cards and pictures and candies and chocolates. Mary Jane thought surely it must be a drug store, it had so many sorts of things. She decided that she would buy her cards here for she liked the look of the place. She sat down by a counter where the cards were spread out and took her time to make selections. Never had she seen such lovely pictures— and they were true ones, too. One showed exactly the view out of her window up at the hotel. She chose two copies of that picture the very first thing.

"I know what you would like—something good?" A soft voice beside her made

Mary Jane turn around to see who was speaking. A motherly looking woman smiled at her and continued, "My man been in the States. He know what little American girl like. A 'soda.'" She rolled the word out proudly. "I give you a soda while you pick out your pictures."

"Will you really?" exclaimed Mary Jane, delightedly. Wouldn't Alice be surprised? Why, they hadn't had a soda all the time they were in Europe! Not one!

The woman disappeared through a door and Mary Jane sat waiting, her mouth actually watering in anticipation. She would like to go for Alice. But if she left, maybe the woman would change her mind. Better stay and get that soda; then fetch Alice and buy another one later, she thought.

In a few minutes the woman returned and proudly set before Mary Jane a glass of—well, something. Mary Jane knew it wasn't a soda—at any rate, not the kind of soda she knew about. But the woman was smiling so happily that Mary Jane didn't dare disappoint her.

"See," she said, "I know what you like. A soda. All little girls in the States like a soda. You drink. I give it to you." And then she broke into a chatter that Mary Jane couldn't understand.

Of course she tasted it—and thought it was terrible!—and it was terrible! The only thing about it like a real American soda was that it was cold. There wasn't any ice cream or rich syrup. But the woman looked on so cordially that—what do you suppose? Mary Jane drank it all down—drinking fast so she wouldn't taste it so much. Then she paid for her postals and said "thank you" as nicely as she knew how and ran to find her mother and sister as fast as ever she could. Going to buy pictures was one thing, but being treated to a soda was quite a different matter.

She waited till they were outside the

shawl shop and started well up the street away from the postal card shop, before she told her experience.

"Mary Jane Merrill!" exclaimed her mother, "You don't mean to say that you've been eating thing, goodness knows where!"

"It wasn't goodness knows where," explained Mary Jane, "it was at the postal card shop and it wasn't things, she called it a soda, Mother. But it wasn't our sort of a soda—not the least our sort."

"I think we'd better go back and see what she had," decided Mrs. Merrill, bothered and puzzled as to what to do. "We'd better know, anyway."

So they went back to the shop and while Mrs. Merrill bought some of the really beautiful cards, Mr. Merrill and Alice ordered sodas. The same woman waited on them and she beamed and smiled at Mary Jane as though they were old friends. Mr. Merrill thought the soda very refreshing.

"You were expecting an American ice

cream soda," he said, "and of course this isn't that. But it's all right anyway, and no harm done, Mother."

"Only I don't want another one," said Mary Jane, positively.

"Then I'll buy you some chocolate and you can take it home and eat it after dinner," said her father when he saw that the kind storekeeper would be too disappointed not to have the little lady get something.

But dear me, after the delicious tea, not even Swiss chocolate seemed interesting. Mary Jane decided to put the package away until later and they strolled on back to the hotel. After dinner they sat on the balcony and watched the lights come out in the town as the sun set back behind the hotel.

"Want to go anywhere or do anything this evening?" asked Mr. Merrill.

"Yes," replied Mrs. Merrill, "I want to take a tram car ride to the top of Mount Brè. I've been watching as that car goes up and down and I want to take the ride, now, while the evening is cool."

"I've been watching it, too," said Mary Jane, "but I'm tired of going to the top of places. Couldn't Alice and I stay here, Mother? We'd be all right. You know this is Switzerland and nothing could happen to us. Everyone is so kind."

Mrs. Merrill looked at the sleepy girls and decided that the suggestion was a. good one. She slipped out to make sure that the kind maid on their floor could come if the girls should need anything and ring. Then with advice not to stay up late, and promising to return inside of two hours, she and Mr. Merrill left.

"Now, Alice," said Mary Jane, "before we go to bed, let's play we are princesses and we are shut up in this castle which is our home. And we've come out on the lookout—that's the balcony—to see over our domains and find if we can send for help."

"I think help's coming now—there's a

train arriving," laughed Alice as the ringing of a bell down at the railroad crossing told them a train would soon pass. The gates dropped at the street crossing and in a few seconds a passenger train arrived from the north, dropping several people at the station. It tooted and went on and the people scattered. The girls couldn't see far because the daylight was fading fast, but they soon noticed two people getting out of the bus at their hotel.

"You might play they are foreign visitors, arriving for a conference," suggested Alice, playfully.

"Or they might be visiting princesses," said Mary Jane. "And Alice! They are! That's Doris! And she's going to stop here!"

She waved frantically at Doris. But she didn't like to shout, and Doris, looking up, couldn't recognize anyone she knew through the iron railing.

"Now I suppose they'll go somewhere

'way off and we won't see them till morning," said Mary Jane, sighing. "And just when we were getting started to play."

She sat very still, watching the lights go up and down over on Mount Brè. Probably by now, her father and mother were on one of those lighted cars. She felt very sleepy and didn't so much care about playing princess.

Suddenly a small voice said, "Mother! Look at this lovely balcony all our own!" And there was Doris—just on the other side of the little railing. Mary Jane jumped up and called to her. The girls were so glad to see each other that you would never have guessed that they had said good-by only three days before. Then Mrs. Dana hadn't known just how long she would be staying in Switzerland, and so the girls hadn't expected to meet again.

"I think we ought to celebrate this reunion," said Mrs. Dana, when she saw how happy the girls were to be together, and heard that they were alone. "Alice, let's you and me give a party. Doris is hungry from the train ride and I know Mary Jane can always eat something. Let's get some chicken sandwiches and cookies—little Swiss cakes, you know, they're lovely. And hot chocolate if you want it—or maybe cold milk? We'll come around to your room if you promised your mother not to leave yours, and we'll have the party as soon as we wash our hands and the food appears."

"I've some chocolate candy we can have," said Mary Jane, remembering the candy of the afternoon.

"Fine!" replied Mrs. Dana, approvingly, "and we have some fruit we brought from the train. Something tells me that nobody is going to starve at this midnight feast. What do you think?"

"I think it's going to be fine, that's what I think," said Mary Jane.

And indeed it was. The sandwiches and cakes came up just as Doris was washed and ready for them. The hot chocolate and a great pitcher full of cold milk arrived soon after with colorful goblets of native pottery on the tray. Doris had the hot chocolate because she was so tired from the journey but the others had milk because it was cool, so everyone was pleased. Mary Jane's candy was so good that they all decided they would have to go back to that same shop in the morning and get a supply before they left Lugano.

The party lasted till Mr. and Mrs. Merrill returned. You can guess how surprised they were to see their visitors and to know that Mary Jane wasn't sleepy a bit, nor lonesome either, she was having such a good time.

"You'll like this place," Mrs. Merrill predicted.

"I'm sure I will," said Mrs. Dana, "and Doris and I are going to stay here for several days and have a nice time playing around."

"But we're leaving tomorrow," exclaimed Mary Jane, in disappointment, "I thought maybe you'd go, too."

"No, not this time," Mrs. Dana replied, "but let's not say good-by again, for there's no telling when we'll run across each other again."

"And have another party like this," added Mary Jane.

"But if certain people I know are to take a ten o'clock train for Italy in the morning, I think they'd better——"

"Be going to bed," laughed Mary Jane, who was getting sleepy again and didn't in the least object to the idea of climbing into that big, comfortable looking bed.

"But be sure to call us in time so we can show Doris the candy and postal shop before we leave," she asked, as she began to undress. Her mother promised that she would.

Next morning the two families had breakfast together and took a walk until train time. Mary Jane would have liked to stay, and then, too, she wanted to go, for good times always were ahead in this trip.

THE MARY JANE SERIES

By CLARA INGRAM JUDSON

Take a trip with Mary Jane. She is the heroine of this popular series for young girls. You'll find her a charming traveling conpanion. Her good nature, her abounding interest in her friends and surroundings, and her fascinating adventures both at home and abroad have endeared her to thousands all over the country.

GROSSET & DUNLAP, Publishers, NEW YORK

THE NANCY DREW MYSTERY STORIES
By CAROLYN KEENE

Illustrated. Every Volume Complete in Itself.

Here is a thrilling series of mystery stories for girls. Nancy Drew, ingenious, alert, is the daughter of a famous criminal lawyer and she herself is deeply interested in his mystery cases. Her interest involves her often in some very dangerous and exciting situations.

THE SECRET OF THE OLD CLOCK
Nancy, unaided, seeks to locate a missing will and finds herself in the midst of adventure.

THE HIDDEN STAIRCASE
Mysterious happenings in an old stone mansion lead to an investigation by Nancy.

THE BUNGALOW MYSTERY
Nancy has some perilous experiences around a deserted bungalow.

THE MYSTERY AT LILAC INN
Quick thinking and quick action were needed for Nancy to extricate herself from a dangerous situation.

THE SECRET AT SHADOW RANCH
On a vacation in Arizona Nancy uncovers an old mystery and solves it.

THE SECRET OF RED GATE FARM
Nancy exposes the doings of a secret society on an isolated farm.

THE CLUE IN THE DIARY
A fascinating and exciting story of a search for a clue to a surprising mystery.

NANCY'S MYSTERIOUS LETTER
Nancy receives a letter informing her that she is heir to a fortune. This story tells of her search for another Nancy Drew.

THE SIGN OF THE TWISTED CANDLES
Nancy, as mediator in a generation-old feud, divulges an unknown birthright.

THE PASSWORD TO LARKSPUR LANE
A carrier pigeon furnishes Nancy with a clue to a mysterious retreat.

THE CLUE OF THE BROKEN LOCKET
Nancy's sympathy for adopted twins leads her into a surprising mystery.

THE MESSAGE IN THE HOLLOW OAK
In Canada, Nancy protects her new property from a crooked promoter.

THE MYSTERY OF THE IVORY CHARM
Nancy solves an Indian mystery by means of a lucky elephant charm.

GROSSET & DUNLAP   *Publishers*   NEW YORK

THE BOBBSEY TWINS BOOKS
FOR LITTLE MEN AND WOMEN
By LAURA LEE HOPE

ILLUSTRATED. *Every volume complete in itself.*

These books for boys and girls between the ages of three and ten stand among children and their parents of this generation where the books of Louisa May Alcott stood in former days. The haps and mishaps of this inimitable pair of twins, their many adventures and experiences are a source of keen delight to imaginative children.

THE BOBBSEY TWINS
THE BOBBSEY TWINS IN THE COUNTRY
THE BOBBSEY TWINS AT THE SEASHORE
THE BOBBSEY TWINS AT SCHOOL
THE BOBBSEY TWINS AT SNOW LODGE
THE BOBBSEY TWINS ON A HOUSEBOAT
THE BOBBSEY TWINS AT MEADOW BROOK
THE BOBBSEY TWINS AT HOME
THE BOBBSEY TWINS IN A GREAT CITY
THE BOBBSEY TWINS ON BLUEBERRY ISLAND
THE BOBBSEY TWINS ON THE DEEP BLUE SEA
THE BOBBSEY TWINS IN WASHINGTON
THE BOBBSEY TWINS IN THE GREAT WEST
THE BOBBSEY TWINS AT CEDAR CAMP
THE BOBBSEY TWINS AT THE COUNTY FAIR
THE BOBBSEY TWINS CAMPING OUT
THE BOBBSEY TWINS AND BABY MAY
THE BOBBSEY TWINS KEEPING HOUSE
THE BOBBSEY TWINS AT CLOVERBANK
THE BOBBSEY TWINS AT CHERRY CORNER
THE BOBBSEY TWINS AND THEIR SCHOOLMATES
THE BOBBSEY TWINS TREASURE HUNTING
THE BOBBSEY TWINS AT SPRUCE LAKE
THE BOBBSEY TWINS WONDERFUL SECRET
THE BOBBSEY TWINS AT THE CIRCUS
THE BOBBSEY TWINS ON AN AIRPLANE TRIP
THE BOBBSEY TWINS SOLVE A MYSTERY
THE BOBBSEY TWINS ON A RANCH
THE BOBBSEY TWINS IN ESKIMO LAND

GROSSET & DUNLAP   :-:   *Publishers*   :-:   NEW YORK

The Little Indian Series
By DAVID CORY

The beauty of Indian legend—the thrill of Indian adventure—the poetry of the Indian's religion, and, above all, perhaps, the sturdy manhood and the idealism of the Indian boy will be an inspiration to every child.

LITTLE INDIAN

The life of Little Indian, on the prairie and in the forest, is full of exciting adventures. His battle with the wildcat that, in the dead of night, attacks his favorite pony; his escape from a band of hostile Indians to the island of the Great Beaver; his pursuit of the red-winged goose and her seven snow-white goslings will thrill and stir the young imagination.

RED FEATHER

"Red Feather" is the warrior name given to "Little Indian." In this story the boy learns some of the secrets of healing and his friends, the animals, teach him the Medicine Song. He goes out on his first big hunt with the braves of the tribe and through his daring and skill wins his war shield. And now, no longer considered a child, he is sent on his first important mission for the tribe.

WHITE OTTER

Red Feather has won the admiration and friendship of everyone but the jealous and cowardly boy, White Otter. This mean-spirited youth seeks every opportunity to harm the son of Big Chief. Thus when Red Feather is sent on an important mission to Three Feathers, chief of a friendly tribe, White Otter follows him. But his plot to harm and disgrace Red Feather fails and the son of Big Chief safely reaches the distant camp.

STAR MAIDEN

Now Red Feather, first known as "Little Indian", has grown to manhood and has proved himself a worthy son of his father Big Chief. But he has to prove himself still further before he wins the heart and hand of lovely Star Maiden. For many moons he strives and at last he brings her to his father's camp where she is welcomed as his bride.

GROSSET & DUNLAP   *Publishers*   NEW YORK

Headline Books for Girls

From 12 to 16 Years

BABS .... *Faith Baldwin*
Another story of Divine Corners, in which the gay venturesome girls get in and out of all sorts of scrapes. But briefly the story tells of the difficulties and thrills Babs encounters in learning to fly.

DAYS OF GOLD .... *Ann Spence Warner*
This story of a forsaken house, a lost diary, a sack of gold dust lying hidden in an abandoned mine, keeps readers tense with surprise and excitement.

JUDY .... *Faith Baldwin*
Judy and her chums explore an island near their summer camp—and find a real mystery to solve.

AT MIDNIGHT .... *Louise Platt Hauck*
A thoroughly puzzling and exciting mystery throws into confusion a group of lovable, high spirited young people.

GOLD IS WHERE YOU FIND IT ......*Ann Spence Warner*
Even in the gold rush area of Cripple Creek, all was not gold that glittered; but Milly found plenty of thrills.

SIDESADDLE RANCH .... *Ann Spence Warner*
A city family tries to make its way on a Colorado ranch.

GROSSET & DUNLAP   *Publishers*   New York

Three Stories of Fun and Friendship

THE MAIDA BOOKS
by INEZ HAYNES IRWIN

MAIDA'S LITTLE SHOP

In a darling little shop of her own Maida makes many friends with the school children who buy her fascinating wares.

MAIDA'S LITTLE HOUSE

All of her friends spend a happy summer in Maida's perfect little house that has everything a child could wish for.

MAIDA'S LITTLE SCHOOL

Three delightful grownups come to visit and the children study many subjects without knowing that they are really "going to school."

GROSSET & DUNLAP   *Publishers*   NEW YORK